SO YOU WANT A SECOND CHANCE

SO YOU WANT TO BE A BILLIONAIRE BOOK 1

ELIZABETH MADDREY

1

He couldn't quite get a breath.

Joseph Robinson pushed back from his desk, checked the time on his Rolex, and stood. He straightened his shoulders, trying to ease the catch that was keeping air from his lungs, and winced. Ouch. He pressed his hand to his chest, then rubbed.

Pain stabbed his heart.

He took one stumbling step, his numb left arm flailing out and hitting the desk as he toppled to the floor. Files tipped and fell, and papers floated to the floor around him.

He should call out.

He tried, but it was weak even to his own ears.

Was this it? The end? After all he'd done, he was going to die on the floor of the office where he'd made his billions.

He was only fifty-five. It wasn't fair.

Or right.

He still had so much more to do.

Joe tried to get up. He tried to crawl to the door where his admin could help.

Another piercing jab of pain, and his head hit the floor.

"Mr. Robinson, you're going to be la—" Marla's shriek was the last thing he heard.

Beep . . . Beep . . . Beep . . .

Joe's eyelids were heavy. His whole body was heavy. Sluggish.

"Mr. Robinson? You're awake. That's good. I'm Nina, one of the nurses who'll be taking care of you until you get transferred out of the ICU."

The voice was female. Brisk. Was it cheerful? Not really.

He worked to push his eyes open and tried to focus on the blurry face beside his bed.

His bed? ICU?

"Don't try to talk." The woman—Nina—smiled before she turned to adjust something out of sight. "I'm sure you have questions. Let's see if I can get you some answers. First, you had a heart attack. Do you remember being in your office? Just nod."

He nodded. It wasn't a crisp memory—but there'd been pain. And he'd fallen. The meeting. He'd missed the meeting. That merger was obviously dead in the water.

"You ended up needing a quadruple bypass. Normally, they would have waited and tried to schedule soon, but things were bad enough that they made the decision to just do it. It worked out well for you. Dr. Mitchell was on call. She's the best." The nurse patted his knee gently before turning to the computer and typing. After a moment she added, "You'll probably stay here with us for a day. Maybe two. Then they'll step you down to the cardiac unit. We will need to get a little more information from you once they get that tube out. You need to update your emergency contact sheet at the office."

Joe watched her, the words spinning through his mind. They should mean more than they did. But everything was foggy.

"Don't worry about it for now. Dr. Mitchell should be around to see you in the next hour or two. Do you want me to let your emergency contact know you're okay? I have that number."

He nodded and tried to force his brain to clear. His admin at work was his emergency contact. Letting her know would get all the appropriate balls rolling. Joe wasn't going to bother his eighty-year-old parents with this. They wouldn't be able to help. Mom's health wasn't great, anyway. She and Dad were better off staying in Florida. Which left work. His admin would get in touch with Tyler Shaw. That was what needed to happen.

Joe relaxed back into the pillow. Tyler would handle things until he got back to work.

"Okay. I'll give them a ring. If you need anything, press this button." Nina indicated the control for the nurse call. "We're always close on this floor."

"Hi, Nina." Another woman, older—closer to his age if the silver in her hair was any indication—strode into the room. She got a couple of squirts of hand sanitizer and rubbed her palms together before reaching for a pair of gloves in the dispenser on the wall. "How are you feeling, Joe?"

Joe blinked. He knew that voice. Mitchell. Dr. Mitchell. Dr. *Cynthia* Mitchell? She stepped to the side of his bed with a warm, if detached, smile. Memories rushed back and the monitor beside him reflected the increase in his heart rate.

"I guess it's not fair to ask you questions when you can't talk because of tubes and machinery." There were little wrinkles at the corners of her eyes. Hadn't someone told him that meant a person smiled a lot? So she was happy, then. That was good. She consulted the computer. "Hmm. We can probably take the tube out. Everything looks like it's okay. You'll still need to take it slow

—that's going to be the keyword for a while. Slow. Which I understand isn't your usual speed."

His thoughts were still foggy, but they were sharpening with Cynthia's presence. She'd been keeping track of him? It certainly sounded like it. And yet, it was unlikely. She'd been clear— they'd both been clear—their goodbye was permanent. No looking back. Those had been her words. And she'd followed through. He'd stood there and watched her walk away.

She'd never once looked back.

Cynthia and Nina talked in low voices over by the computer. Joe couldn't quite make out the words. He was drifting—his eyelids heavy. He let them close.

A hand shook his shoulder.

"Joe?"

He opened his eyes. Cynthia's face was closer now. He could see the fine lines and the hint of freckles under her face powder.

She smiled. "I'll let you sleep in just a couple of minutes. I want you to take a deep breath and exhale through your mouth."

Joe breathed in. As he let the air out, Cynthia tugged the breathing tube free.

He coughed. It hurt.

"Good. Take it slow and breathe again. In and out, just like that." Cynthia nodded as Joe breathed. She checked some of the tubes that ran from his body to the machines nearby. "Your O2 looks good. You can have a small sip of water, if you want?"

He nodded again, not quite trusting his voice when his throat was this raw. He took the cup and straw she offered and sipped. Cold water had never tasted so good. "Thanks."

"My pleasure. Nina says she told you about your surgery. I imagine you have some questions?"

Joe had a lot of questions.

All of them were about his heart.

Very few of them had to do with his health.

CYNTHIA TOSSED her white coat over the back of the chair in front of her desk and rolled her shoulders.

Joe Robinson.

She shook her head and moved behind her desk to sign in to her computer. Coming back to the DC area had always held the risk of running into him again.

She'd thought she'd been prepared.

She wasn't supposed to be the on-call today, but George had needed to swap for a family emergency, and she'd agreed. It wasn't as though she had anything else more pressing right now. Her condo overlooking Tyson's Corner was as decorated as it was likely to get, and the majority of her belongings were unpacked. She could have spent the day rearranging things— had planned to—but working was always better.

A knock, then an impossibly young head poking through the doorway. "Dr. Mitchell?"

"Dr. Curtis." She waved him in. "What can I do for you?"

"I was wondering if I could ask a few questions about the quad earlier today?"

Joe. Of course. Dr. Curtis was a resident and had been a good help in the OR. "Sure."

Dr. Curtis sat in the chair opposite her and folded his hands on his knees. "I heard somewhere that you knew the patient."

"News travels fast," she murmured.

"Nurses . . . I guess Nina picked up on something and the patient—Mr. Robinson—answered her questions." He shrugged. "I was just wondering if that made it harder."

Her eyebrows lifted. Hard*er*. "Was it hard?"

"Well, it's a complicated surgery and there are so many risks . . ."

"That's true. But that's true of most cardiac procedures. You want cardiology, don't you?"

He bit his lower lip. "I guess I'm not sure now."

"Because of today's operation?" Cynthia sorted through the procedure. What had set him off? There weren't really many textbook heart surgeries, but Joe's bypass had been as close as she'd been in a while. "What aspect of it?"

Dr. Curtis shrugged.

She'd leave it, for now, and answer the question he'd asked. But it was something she'd need to follow up on. If he wanted this specialty, he'd need to toughen up. "I haven't seen Joe in more than thirty years. So while I knew him, a long time ago, I don't know him now."

He nodded slowly. "So it wasn't harder?"

"No. He was a patient who needed my expertise. That's all anyone under your care can be. You have to be able to separate yourself from the patients and maintain empathy and compassion. It can be a fine line, but the best doctors find it and learn to walk on it."

The chatter in the hall outside was the only sound. Nurses called to one another. Gurneys rolled past as they were moved from place to place whether empty or full. Cynthia studied Dr. Curtis. He was a promising resident.

She sighed. "You are a wonderful doctor. You're going to be an asset to whatever specialty you choose, but you're going to need to make that decision and stick. Even if it's harder than you thought it would be."

"I know that. I do." He nodded. "I want cardiology. I don't know what about today was so unsettling."

"Spend some time thinking about it, and if you figure it out and want to talk again, come back. From a clinical standpoint, it went exactly as it should have. He's an otherwise healthy, middle-aged male. His prognosis is excellent. He'll need to make some lifestyle changes, but otherwise, once he's fully recovered, there's no reason to anticipate any problems." Cynthia pressed her lips together. Joe making lifestyle changes was a concern. If he hadn't mellowed with age—and nothing she'd read about him in the last thirty-plus years suggested he had—change wasn't going to be something he embraced.

"I will. Thank you, Dr. Mitchell."

"Anytime." She smiled as the young resident stood and left her office, then turned back to her computer. Everything she'd said about professional distance from Joe's case was a lie. She prayed and quickly asked forgiveness—and for understanding. Because she thought she and God had made a deal when she'd walked away from Joe all those years ago. It had been the hardest thing she'd done in her life—and she'd finished a pre-med degree in three years, so she'd been no stranger to hard things.

It had also been right.

That still wasn't a question.

The Joe she'd loved in college had been bright, determined, and all-in when it came to his goals to take the tech world by storm. He'd done that and then some. Cynthia was proud of him. And sure, maybe there was that small part of her that wondered—only occasionally—if they wouldn't have been able to make it work.

But she hadn't been successful with a relationship since him. So why would anything with Joe, a man who'd been just as goal-oriented as she was, have been different? If anything, it would have ended in the type of volcanic explosion that left scars and debris that never really went away.

Cynthia nodded her head and pushed personal thoughts aside. She'd give herself a moment, later tonight, when she was ensconced in her home and away from the office, to weep a little for Joe and the love that still haunted her dreams. Right now it was time to concentrate on her patients—and on the changes she was going to have to convince Joe to make so he didn't end up on her table again.

Because no matter how completely over him she was, Cynthia wasn't going to be able to handle working on his heart a second time.

2

"I still don't see why I can't have my laptop." Joe scowled at the nurse standing by the computer she'd wheeled into the room with her. "Lying in this bed is going to drive me batty. Don't you care about my mental health, too?"

"There's a TV remote attached to the bed. You're allowed to get up and walk the halls."

Joe grunted. He was allowed to walk the halls once every couple of hours. Even then, "allowed" wasn't the word he'd choose. Forced. Coerced. Tortured. The fact that it left him exhausted and near collapse was beside the point. As was the brain fog that lingered at the edges of his mind. Those were limitations he didn't choose to accept. "I have work."

"Your work is to heal. You had major surgery. From what I see here, you're lucky to be alive. Maybe you should spend some time thinking about why the Good Lord saw fit to keep you on this Earth. That ought to take up some of your time." There was the hint of a chuckle in the nurse's voice. "I ordered your lunch for you. Dr. Mitchell should be in to see you in the next hour or so, too. You ask her about your laptop. If she gives the go-ahead, no one's going to stop you. For now, I'm taking the machine back to the nurses station with me and locking it up."

"You can leave it here."

Now she did chuckle. "Mmmhmm. 'Cause you're sure to leave it alone when no one's looking. Nice try, honey. I've been on the cardiac floor for more than ten years. I know your type. Ask the doctor."

Joe recognized the look of finality on her face and bit back another objection. He had work, darn it. Cynthia had better approve his laptop use or . . . he sighed. Or what? He had no power in this situation. He was hooked up to more machines than he was going to take the time to count. And maybe he hurt in ways he hadn't known were possible. But his brain was fine, if foggy. And even foggy, his brain was what his workplace needed right now.

He hadn't been out of contact with the office for going on three days in . . . ever.

Maybe that was part of what had landed him here.

"You push that call button if you need anything." The nurse stopped and pointed at him. "Anything *other* than your laptop."

Joe gave a short laugh and nodded. "Fine."

"That's more like it." With that parting shot, the nurse was out the door, and he was alone with the TV.

Joe frowned at the blank screen. He wasn't about to start watching soap operas and talk shows. Or the commercials aimed at bored, stay-at-home women and the elderly. Did they have movie channels?

He turned it on and started to scroll. His eyes got heavier with each press of the button.

"Joe?" Someone touched his hand.

That voice. He knew that voice. Joe dragged himself through the grogginess that was plaguing him and opened his eyes. "Cyn."

She smiled. "No one's called me that in a long time. How are you feeling?"

How *was* he feeling? Joe closed his eyes and took stock. "Achy. Bored."

"I heard about that." Cynthia's eyes crinkled at the corners when she grinned. "I'm not sure about the laptop just yet. But let's take a look and see."

"Don't the machines tell you everything?"

Cynthia shook her head and lightly rested her stethoscope against his chest. With a satisfied nod, she hooked it back around her neck. "Can I check your incisions?"

"Yeah. You're the doctor."

She laughed. "So I am. I will admit that when I found out I was getting the position here, I thought about giving you a call to see if you wanted to get a cup of coffee. I was not so desperate to see you that I wanted you on my operating table."

"Not exactly my plan, either. I don't understand it. I'm healthy. I exercise every day. Eat right."

"Mmm." She twitched the covers off his legs and checked the incisions.

"That explains why my legs hurt."

"We grafted veins from your legs to your heart. So yes, incisions there as well as the one from the open-heart surgery. The legs will heal faster than your chest. Everything looks good." She settled the blanket back over him and clasped her hands. "What about stress?"

"What about it?"

"How much stress do you have, Joe?"

How was he supposed the measure that? "Is there a scale? Like the pain one, maybe?"

"You were always a joker. Let's try it this way. How many hours a day do you work?"

He looked away, staring out the hospital room window at the side of the building next to them.

"Come on, Joe. I can't help you if you don't help me."

He sighed. "I don't know. What counts as working? I'm in the office ten or eleven hours most days."

"And how much work do you take home?"

"Depends. There's always something more to do." And even if he didn't take a specific project home, he couldn't exactly leave his brain in the office. He was going to think about problems and chew over solutions.

She shook her head. "You still allergic to sleeping?"

"I get six hours a night. Seven on Saturdays, since I can sleep in a little on Sunday mornings."

"And for fun? What are your hobbies? Who are your friends? How do you relax and get away from it all?" Cynthia crossed her arms.

Joe shrank under her piercing stare. "I have friends."

"I can see they're very concerned about you."

She'd always had a way with dry, sharp sarcasm. Joe smiled. "Yeah, well. I'm sure they would be if they knew."

"Who does know you're here?"

"My admin. I imagine she told the board and a few key employees. There's a protocol." He hated the defensiveness in his voice. He wasn't doing anything wrong here. He'd had a heart attack. Why was she being so harsh?

"And your wife? Or girlfriend?"

"I don't have either of those. You always said I was married to my work. When you left, I figured maybe you had the right idea."

She frowned. "You've dated."

"Have I?"

Pink stained her cheeks. "I've seen the write-ups. It's natural to follow the career of someone you knew who went on to do great things. Some of the women on your arm have been very glamorous."

"I almost hate to tell you the truth." Joe shook his head. "Most of the time, those were dates arranged by my admin. It doesn't do to show up to the charity galas single, so she'd drum someone up."

"Like . . . escorts?" The shock on her face was almost comical.

He held up a hand. "No, no, no. Like friends of friends. People who wanted to go but couldn't afford the ticket. I'd buy them a dress and some accessories and get them into the event, and they'd pose on my arm on the red carpet. Win-win."

"Still sounds like an escort. Just an unofficial one."

"Sorry to disappoint. Though I don't know that we know each other well enough for you to disapprove. How's *Mister* Dr. Mitchell?" Who was he? There had been plenty of guys who gave Cynthia the eye when she'd been with him. The jealousy returned like an old friend. Or a bad case of hives.

"You're not the only one married to their career." She huffed out a breath. "So I guess I can't throw stones. The point I was trying to make is that you have a lot of stress in your life—you work constantly, and even with your version of eating healthy and exercising, it's not uncommon for heart problems to happen. Especially given your family history."

Joe closed his eyes. Of course she knew about that. She'd been by his side when he'd rushed to his mother's hospital room. That heart attack was part of the reason his parents had moved out of the area to Florida. Dad said it was their wakeup call. Maybe this was his.

"How is your mom?"

"She's great, Cyn. No more episodes—that's what she's taken to calling it, an episode. She and Dad live in Florida in a neighborhood filled with retirees. They're some of the older folks on the block, but the younger ones—you know, the kids in their early seventies—look in on them. They love it."

"Have you called them?"

He shook his head. "No. I figured I'd wait until I was home so I wouldn't have to lie when I said I was fine."

"You need to call them today, Joe. They deserve to know."

"They'll just want to come."

"So fly them up. You have a plane."

Three of them, though that didn't seem to be worth mentioning. He could send a driver to collect them and get them to the airstrip. Fly them up. Have someone else ferry them around here so he didn't have to worry about them on the roads. "I don't know."

"They're your parents and they love you. They do still love you?"

"They do." His shoulders drooped. "I'll arrange it after you leave. It'd be easier if I had my laptop."

She snorted and shook her head. "You're incorrigible. Fine. I'll get you your laptop, since you went to the trouble of having it dropped off, but I'm also giving the nurses instructions to keep the charging cable at their station and to limit the time you spend on it. You get three hours of laptop time a day while you're in my unit."

"But—"

Cynthia held up her hand. "Don't try to fight me on this. Right now? What I say, goes."

It was better than nothing. Barely. "Yes, Dr. Mitchell."

She flashed a grin. "That's better. I'll go get your machine. I'm serious, though. I expect to see your parents when I do rounds tomorrow."

"I'm still going to be here tomorrow?" He frowned. "I thought maybe I'd get to go home."

"Not today. Not tomorrow. Depending on how well you behave, we can talk about the day after that. Be right back."

Joe watched Cynthia stride from his room. She walked fast—always had—and didn't waste excess movement. She was exactly the same as she'd been in college. Just a little older. A little more experienced.

His feelings were exactly the same as they'd been in college, too.

And probably just as fruitless.

He was still married to his work, and Cynthia Mitchell still had impressive plans to save the world.

CYNTHIA CHECKED in at the nurses station before starting down the hallway to Joe's room. She'd had to force herself not to visit him more than her other patients. Her heart might want to give him preferential treatment, but her ethics had kept her in line. Maybe she ought to spring him a day early.

Laughter floated down the hall from his room.

She smiled. Their voices were older, but she still recognized them. She knocked on the doorframe before stepping through and around the privacy curtain that shielded the room from the doorway. "Knock knock. Mr. and Mrs. Robinson, it's so good to see you."

"Cynthia? Oh, honey, it's you." Joe's mom turned to beam at her son. "Is this the surprise you were hinting about?"

"Yes, Mom. I thought you'd get a kick out of it."

Cynthia crossed the room and gave Mrs. Robinson a quick hug. The woman's shoulders were thinner, frailer, than she remembered, but the scent of lilac was the same. She moved to Joe's dad and repeated the process, her nose filling with hints of sawdust and basil.

"How are you feeling today, Joe?" Cynthia pushed some buttons on the machines beside her patient and considered the information. He was doing well.

"Ready to go home."

"Oh, Joe." Mrs. Robinson patted his knee. "You were always one to rush things. Look where that got you. You need to stay here until Dr. Mitchell says you're ready."

"Listen to your mother." Mr. Robinson winked at Cynthia. "Besides, you've got this lovely doctor looking in on you. Why would you want to give that up?"

Joe chuckled and looked over at Cynthia. Their eyes met, and her breath caught in her throat.

No. No, no, no, no, no! She was not getting lost in those eyes again. Joe Robinson was her *patient,* and that was all. She wasn't going down that rabbit trail again. She curved her lips into what she prayed was a professional smile. "Tomorrow, for sure. But you're going to need some help at home for a week, maybe two."

"That's why we're here, dear." Mrs. Robinson looked between Joe and Cynthia with a sad, knowing smile. "And if we can't handle it, we'll see to it that he hires someone."

"That might be best. I'll make sure you have a list of providers with your discharge papers. He's steady on his feet, but he still needs to be careful and not push himself too hard." She frowned. "I'd like you to keep to the one battery rule when it comes to work. At least for another week."

"But—"

"We'll make sure he does." Mrs. Robinson sent Joe a quelling look. "His company's a well-oiled machine. They'll be okay without him managing every detail for another week."

"You don't know that," Joe grumbled under his breath.

Cynthia grinned. "I'll ease up on the phone call restrictions, if you promise not to overdo. Think of it as a way to test out your management team and make sure they're competent."

He sighed and closed his eyes. "Fine. I can afford to pay some spies."

"That's the spirit, son." Mr. Robinson's laugh was full and loud. "Nothing says you trust your team like hiring spies."

Joe's cheeks pinked.

Interesting. Cynthia hadn't figured that Joe put stock in anyone's opinion. It was good to know his parents still mattered.

"Besides, you're coming up on your fifty-sixth birthday. Don't you think it's time you started thinking about the next chapter?" Mr. Robinson touched Joe's arm. "You're not going to live forever. This little incident should have made that clear."

Little incident? Cynthia snorted and tried to cover by turning it into a cough.

"I heard that." Joe frowned at her.

"Well. I do have to come down on the side of saying this qualified as a tad more than a 'little incident.' It was part of my oath when I graduated medical school."

Mrs. Robinson chuckled. "I suppose that means I can't call my own heart attacks episodes any longer?"

"Attacks? Plural?" Cynthia glanced at Mrs. Robinson then back at Joe. "I thought you said she'd only had the one."

"That's what I thought." Joe's brows lifted. "Something you need to tell me, Mom?"

"They were nothing." She waved a hand. "Your father and I didn't want to worry you."

"You didn't—I—Dad?" The monitor beside Joe's bed beeped faster as Joe glared at his father.

"Calm down, son. Take a deep breath." Mr. Robinson nodded toward the beeping equipment. "I realize you're upset. They were blips. Mom's cardiologist in Florida is keeping an eye on her and says things are under control."

"It is useful information to know for Joe's medical history." Cynthia paused and watched as Joe got his labored breathing under control. "You're also going to need to work on regulating your emotions. I'll get you some information on yoga and meditation."

"Oh, now, honey." Mrs. Robinson shook her head vigorously. "That's all hooey and the next thing to giving up on Jesus."

Cynthia didn't bother to sigh. She'd had this conversation with a number of patients—or their families—who didn't believe a person could do yoga and still believe in Jesus. "Actually, meditation is a lot like prayer—I spend time every morning reading through a collection of Psalms that help me focus my mind and heart on Christ. It's calming and helps me maintain control. Yoga is a series of stretching exercises with deep breathing associated with them. It's something I do daily as well. Usually right after my Bible study. I put on praise music and use it as an extension of my focused time with Jesus. It doesn't have to be clanging gongs and incense."

Mr. Robinson gave a slight nod. "Slip the information into that discharge packet. We'll give it a look. Maybe you could include the list of Psalms you enjoy?"

"Sure." It was more personal than she would normally allow. But this was Joe—and his parents. Mrs. Robinson might not be her patient, but Cynthia still cared about the woman's health. "I should get going to check on my other patients. You're going to need to set up some follow-up appointments, Joe, with whomever you're choosing as your long-term cardiologist."

"Isn't that you?" Joe reached out and grabbed her wrist. "Can't that be you?"

Cynthia struggled against the familiar warmth that came with Joe's touch. She swallowed. There was no reason Joe couldn't be her patient. She was new to the practice and had the smallest load right now. If he called and asked for an appointment without stating a doctor preference, chances were he'd get assigned to her, anyway.

But she'd held out a tiny sliver of hope that he'd understand he needed to go somewhere else.

"Of course. Call the office when you're home, and they'll get things scheduled." Her duty as a physician was to fix Joe's heart —even if it was going to shatter hers.

Again.

3

"C'mon, Joe. You can go to church. Dr. Mitchell even said it was good for you to move around and get out, provided you took it slow." Mom plunked her hands on her hips and frowned at him.

Joe tugged the sheet up and shook his head. "Mom."

"Joe."

There was no point in even groaning. Once Mom got that tone, she wasn't going to budge. Which meant he was headed to church. He usually watched something online. Or, if he was being honest, had it open in a browser behind whatever work he was doing. It wasn't like he needed to *see* the service to listen.

And okay, fine, maybe he didn't listen as intently as he should when he did it that way. It didn't mean he didn't still love Jesus. He was just busy.

Wasn't there something in the Bible about work being good?

"All right. I'm coming." He shifted, slowly, and sat up, sliding his legs over the edge of the bed. Everything ached. Everything took more time than it should. This was stupid. "I need a shower."

"Of course. I'll go get your father." Mom bustled from the room.

With a sigh, Joe stood and glared at the walker his mom had left within easy reach. He didn't need it. He wasn't old. He wasn't disabled. He started toward the bathroom and was most of the way there before his dad arrived.

"How do you want me to help you?" Dad tucked his hands in the pockets of his slacks.

"Could you just be near in case I call? I can do this." He'd been showering on his own since he was six. Surely almost fifty years of experience would keep him safe?

"Remember to stand with your back to the spray."

Right. So the water didn't pound on his healing incisions. He was also supposed to take fewer than ten minutes in the shower, which ruined the purpose as far as he was concerned. Showers were for lingering. Thinking. Clearing his head. Or at least they had been. When he'd bought this house in Georgetown, he'd been pleased with the renovations the prior owner had made. The en suite of the master bedroom had taken over what used to be another, smaller bedroom.

Joe barely noticed the gleaming marble as he made his way to the oversized shower and spun the handle to turn on the water. He tossed the pajama pants he'd slept in toward the hamper and frowned when they fell short by several feet. Apparently, his aim was still recovering, too.

With his back to the shower head, he eased beneath the warm rainfall and closed his eyes. This, at least, felt normal.

Normal wasn't something he'd had a lot of in the last week. Even work email was different—as if everyone was tiptoeing around lest they be responsible for another heart attack.

Joe eyed the incisions on his chest and leg as he washed. All things considered, they were small reminders of how close he'd come to meeting Jesus in person.

As much as he loved God, Joe wasn't in a hurry to start living with Him full time.

He turned off the shower and reached for his towel.

"You okay? Need me?" Dad's head poked through the bathroom doorway.

"No, Dad. I'm fine." Joe wrapped the towel around his waist and stepped over to the vanity. What church should he take his parents to? When he'd bought this house, he'd always meant to find a congregation in the city. But it was easier to attend online. Or let it slide. "Give me a few minutes to put some clothes on and I'll let Harold know we need him to bring the car around."

His dad nodded and eased out of the room.

Dressing took more energy than it used to. Everything did. Joe scowled at himself in the mirror. This wasn't any part of his five-, ten-, or fifteen-year plan. He had work to do.

Fixing a smile on his face, he stepped out of his bedroom and made his way downstairs to the kitchen. His mother was flipping pancakes onto a plate.

"Sit down, honey, and eat. There should be time." Mom slid the plate onto the long stretch of granite. "Dad went to talk to Harold."

Joe winced. "Harold's kind of protective of the garage. He considers it his domain."

"I'm sure. But you know your father. He can make a friend of anyone."

That was true. It was a skill Joe had learned early. It had served him well in business. He sliced a pie-shaped wedge of pancake and bit in. He pressed his lips together as the unexpected taste hit. They were like glue. He swallowed. "New recipe?"

"Buckwheat." Mom grinned. "I've been reading up on heart-healthy recipes. They're not bad, do you think?"

"They're interesting." It was the best he could manage. They might climb up to "not bad" if he could slather them with butter and drown them in syrup.

"Eat up." She patted his arm as she slid onto a stool beside him. "Tell me about the church you're taking us to."

"About that."

She smiled and nodded toward the plate.

Joe nudged it away from him. "I'm really not hungry. And I think we should probably get going. It's a bit of a drive."

Mom's eyebrows winged up. "You don't attend here in town?"

"No. The church I went to when I first started out— remember I was living closer to Springfield?"

She nodded.

"It's a good church. Solid. You'll like Pastor Brown."

Mom studied him for a long moment. "You never drive all that way each week."

"Well, they stream their service, too. So—"

"You put it on in the background and work." Her lips thinned. "Joseph Andrew Robinson, we raised you better than that."

He hung his head. Fifty-five years old and his mother could still make him feel like a little boy with his hand caught in the cookie jar. Excuses, explanations, and rationalizations clogged in his throat. He looked up at her and swallowed them back down, just like he had as a child. The reality was, she was right. And the look on her face told him she knew it. "Yes, ma'am."

Her lips curved as she leaned over to press her lips to his cheek. "If you're not going to eat, why don't we head on out to the garage? Maybe on the way home from church we can stop somewhere for lunch."

He'd send his chef a quick text from the car. Given that he hadn't been around for breakfast, it was likely Mom had already given him the day—or the week—off. But it was better to make it official. And reassure him that he'd still be paid. "I'd like that."

CYNTHIA SETTLED into the seat of what had become her typical spot in the sanctuary. She nodded to the familiar faces around her. She didn't know names yet, but she was working on it. She couldn't always make it to church, even though she'd been clear that Sundays off were a priority. At least Pastor Brown's sermons were available online. Or she could stream the service if she needed. Or come on Saturday night, though it never felt the same to her. There was something about being in church on Sunday morning that soothed her more than any of the other options.

Today, she needed soothing more than usual.

Joe Robinson.

God sure had a sense of humor.

"Are these seats taken?"

Cynthia glanced up at the voice and laughed when her gaze landed on Joe's dad. "No. Mr. Robinson, it's good to see you again."

His eyes crinkled at the corners as he grinned. "For such a large area, Northern Virginia is sure a small world."

"Mom. I'm not an invalid."

"You kind of are." Cynthia stood and leaned around Joe's dad to watch Joe push himself out of a wheelchair and step away. "I'm glad to see you didn't walk the whole way from the parking lot. It's a big campus."

"Harold dropped us at the front door." He scowled at his mom over his shoulder. "Mom insisted on the chair. I would've been fine. And I'm not sitting in that thing through the service."

"No one said you had to." Mrs. Robinson's voice was calm with a hint of irritation running through the bottom. "I'll just fold it and tuck it over by the wall."

"Let me do that." Cynthia rose and slid past Joe and his dad, who'd both taken their seats. "You sit down, Mrs. Robinson. I'm glad he has you looking out for him."

"Thank you, dear." Mrs. Robinson patted Cynthia's cheek.

Cynthia blew out a breath as she rolled the wheelchair to an out-of-the-way spot. What were the chances? She snorted. Maybe the better question was what was God doing? Because the chances were too slim for this to be anything other than divine intervention. But why?

She walked back to the row. Joe's mom had taken the seat where Cynthia had been sitting, leaving the aisle—the chair beside Joe—open. Her purse and Bible sat neatly on the seat.

"We thought that would be easier for you than climbing over everyone." Mrs. Robinson sent her an innocent smile.

Cynthia didn't buy it for a minute, but she forced her lips upward. "Thanks."

"Wasn't my idea." Joe's mutter was barely loud enough for her to hear over the opening guitar strums as the worship band moved into place on stage. "I can get them to move, if you want. I'm sorry about this."

"It's fine, Joe." She turned to study him as he gripped the chair in front of him and stood. His color was better—it would have to be, since he was still alive and kicking—but he still had the look of someone who'd been seriously ill. And he still made everything in her yearn. Why hadn't thirty years taken care of that? She waited until he glanced her way. "We said we'd be friends. Distance and workload meant we never had to test it out until now, but I'd still like to give it a shot. Especially since we're going to be seeing a lot of each other for a while."

He nodded. "I'd like that, too."

"Good." She touched his arm, just briefly, and regretted it immediately. He shouldn't still have that effect on her—but he did. And no one in the last thirty years had ever come close. But it seemed like he didn't feel the same, which was exactly how it should be. Thirty years was a long time to be in love with someone who was out of reach. Cynthia watched his eyes as he smiled at her, the little wrinkles in the corners a less-defined mirror of his dad's.

With effort, Cynthia turned toward the front and joined in on the chorus. She was at church to praise Jesus and learn, not to moon over Joe Robinson. She'd done enough of that already for one lifetime. She was older now. Smarter. And she had a fulfilling life. Maybe it wasn't exactly the life she'd dreamed of, but not all fairytales came true. She was, without a doubt, doing what God wanted her to do. So she'd rest in that and be content.

What other choice was there?

Cynthia dragged her thoughts away from Joe and focused on the service.

When Pastor Brown invited everyone to rise for the benediction, she glanced over at Joe. He looked tired. It wasn't surprising. He'd had major surgery. She probably should have been more clear that moving around didn't really mean going to church, but she hadn't thought Joe still attended. She'd always felt that she'd been the one dragging him to any of events and services they'd gone to in college. He hadn't fought it, but he hadn't been the one to bring it up, either.

Maybe his faith had deepened with time, like hers had.

Or maybe his parents had dragged him here today.

She wanted to know who Joe was now and compare it to who he'd been when they'd sat on the grass in the quad and planned their futures together. So much had changed. Was it possible that anything had stayed the same?

Joe sank back onto his seat as recorded music from a popular Christian band played over the speakers. It wasn't the recessional music of days gone by, that was for sure, but Cynthia liked it.

"You feeling okay?"

"Tired. Who knew sitting in church could be exhausting?"

Cynthia raised her hand with a chuckle. "You had major surgery. This was probably a little bit too much."

He nodded and glanced at his parents, who were chatting with the family on the other side of them. "I promised I'd take them to lunch on the way home. I don't imagine you'd want to join us?"

Her eyebrows lifted. "You don't?"

"I . . . well . . . would you?"

His baffled expression made her smile. "As it turns out, I like lunch. And really any meal where food is served. And I wouldn't mind keeping an eye on you if you're going to insist on doing that before heading home and napping."

Joe winced. "I don't want to nap."

"But you need to." She rested her hand on his arm and fought the surge of attraction. "You can't power your way through this recovery, Joe."

He sighed. "I know. That doesn't mean I have to like it."

"Fair enough. I'll go get your wheelchair while you thank your mom for insisting on it and figure out where we're going to eat so I know where to meet you." She gave his arm a light squeeze before weaving through the crowd. Should she have said no? Maybe. There were professional lines and boundaries that she was crossing—had crossed—and yet she couldn't stop herself.

Joe Robinson was back in her life, at least for a little while.

Joe eased out of the car and turned to his driver. "Thanks, Harold. I'll give you a call when the appointment's finished."

"Sounds good. You sure you shouldn't have let your mom come with you? I know she wanted to."

Joe frowned. The downside of having a casual, open relationship with staff was that they became friends. And then they apparently felt they could offer advice in any area of life. "I'm sure. It's been nine days. They're going to head home this weekend, anyway. I need to be able to do things on my own."

Harold raised his eyebrows. "That so?"

"You know what I mean. I'm getting behind in my work, and deadlines are slipping. It's time to find my way back to normal, and I can't do that if my mom is hovering over me like I'm a child."

Harold chuckled. "All right. She made me promise to ask."

"I bet she did." Joe shook his head. "I'll tell her you did your job. Thanks."

"Don't mention it. And Joe?"

"Yeah?"

"I'm glad you lived through this."

"Me, too." He lifted a hand to wave before he started into the medical building. It was easy to forget that his staff—the people who were around him more than anyone else—considered him family. He felt the same, but it was easy to take everything for granted. Harold had been worried. His housekeeper, Doris, had already given him chapter and verse, while making sure he understood that what she said went for Mario, the chef, as well. He signed in at the receptionist's desk and took a seat.

"Mr. Robinson? If you could fill out some paperwork?" The perky blonde behind the counter slid a clipboard his way.

He stood to collect it and returned to his seat. Hadn't he done all of this online before he came?

When the paperwork was filled out—again—he carried the clipboard back up to the desk. The receptionist smiled. "Dr. Mitchell should be with you in just a minute."

Before he could get back to his seat, another door opened to reveal Cynthia, looking smart in dark slacks and a striped shirt. "Hi, Joe. Come on back."

Joe stepped through the door, and his heart gave an extra thump. Cynthia Mitchell still had everything he wanted in a woman. She might be older now, more mature, but she was the real deal. And it was still a terrible idea.

Neither of them was that different than they'd been when they were in college. Oh, sure, little things had changed, but at their core, they were both completely focused on their careers. He had only to look around the walls of her office to confirm it.

Diplomas and awards in mahogany frames adorned an entire wall. Underneath the window and covering the other long wall were bookcases full of thick medical tomes. All were evidence of her commitment to her profession.

"I didn't realize you were this impressive." Joe smiled as he settled in one of the chairs across from her desk.

Cynthia laughed. "You'll find almost all the same stuff in every office in the practice. People who want to continue in cardiology have to stay on top of things. But thank you—I'm assuming there was a compliment in there somewhere."

His face heated. "Of course there was."

"Let's talk about lifestyle changes, shall we?"

"Do we have to?"

Her gaze sharpened and she pressed her lips together. "We do. Your mother isn't with you?"

"No. I don't need a keeper."

"Hmm."

"I don't. Mom and Dad will be heading home at the end of the week, anyway. They have a life, and I'm not going to keep them from it." Besides which he didn't need Mom hovering over him, working herself up. The very last thing he wanted was to cause another heart issue for her because she was worrying about him.

Cynthia shook her head. "I don't suppose I can talk you out of that?"

"No. Look, Cyn—do I need to call you Dr. Mitchell?"

"Given our history, I'll allow the first name, but if you could try to keep it professional when we're around others, I'd appreciate it."

"Of course. Mom's not handling this well, and Dad's worrying about her. It's better all around if they're back home where she can relax and maintain her routine. I have staff at home who are more than happy to keep a close watch on me. Added to all of that, I'm not an idiot. I'm not in a hurry to die, so I understand some things will have to change. I don't think you and I are going to completely agree, but I also think we ought to be able to come to a compromise that we'll both be okay with."

She smiled. "And now I see firsthand one of the reasons

you're so successful. All right, let's negotiate. You need to cut back the hours you work."

"I—" Joe broke off when she raised her hand.

"I didn't say retire or quit or anything like that. In fact, there's no reason you can't work forty or fifty hours each week, provided you're taking frequent breaks and moving around."

Fifty hours was a big downgrade. He averaged closer to a hundred. "That's close to half. You realize that, right?"

Her eyebrows lifted. "No. I guess we see one reason you had heart problems. How many hours of sleep do you get a night now that you're home from the hospital?"

"I don't know. Six?"

"Are you waking with an alarm or naturally?"

"A mixture of both."

She drummed her fingers on her desk. "I'll suggest eighty working hours as an upper limit, but I encourage you to try and get below it. And you should also be trying to get seven or eight hours of sleep. Now, regular exercise."

"I run for an hour every day."

She tilted her head to the side. "Every day?"

"Maybe not every day." He frowned. It was on his schedule— usually he took time at lunch to run. Except lately, meetings had been creeping in and pushing back other work. "I guess I might have been letting that slip lately."

"How long?"

The video game company he'd acquired almost two years ago had come to him with a lot of problems. Most were caused by mismanagement, but they'd also had some internal sabotage. He'd been handling the repair personally. And that had added a lot of work to his already heavy schedule. He cleared his throat. "I guess about two years."

"Right. So, as I was saying, regular exercise. In addition to getting up and moving every hour when you're behind your desk."

He opened his mouth to object but closed it when he caught the look in her eye. One of the most important aspects of negotiation was understanding when someone was dead set against a change. "Okay."

Her eyebrows lifted, but she didn't comment on his easy capitulation. Cynthia glanced down at her checklist. "Diet. We need to evaluate what you're eating and make some changes to be sure that we can get your cholesterol back to where it needs to be. Exercise will help, but it's not the only thing. You don't cook."

"No." Joe shook his head. "I have a chef at home, but I don't eat at home all that often. Business lunches are usually catered, dinners at restaurants—you know how it is."

"I don't, actually." She sighed. "Joe, you're going to have to pay attention. I can send meal plans and suggestions home with you, but that's only going to matter if you have them implemented."

"Mom made buckwheat pancakes. I'm not convinced dying is worse than eating those again."

She laughed. "It's not that bad. I'll give you the information. Will you promise to try?"

"Yeah. I'll give it a try."

"Great. Let's head into an exam room and take a look at how everything is healing."

He looked at her. All those years between them—what could have been? Would it have been possible for the two of them to figure out a way to make it work? To have each other and, possibly, a family? He'd made his company into a family in some ways, but looking back, it wasn't quite the same.

∽

CYNTHIA BENT DOWN and picked up her shoes. It was always good to get home after a long day and finally relax. She had a weekend with nothing ahead of her, barring emergencies, of course. But one major benefit of this new practice—and the main thing that had tipped the scales for her to move to DC and to close down her individual office in the first place—was having enough staff that when doctors were supposed to be off, they were.

Her cell rang as she walked through her condo toward her bedroom. With a frown, she answered. "This is Dr. Mitchell."

"Cynthia? It's Joe. Robinson."

"Are you okay?" There was little reason for a patient to call her personal number, even though she tended to write it on all the various paperwork. Most people called the office and asked to be forwarded—or they dialed 9-1-1 because it was an emergency. But Joe wasn't the only person who skipped all of that. He was just the only one who made her heart rate pick up. Which was stupid. This was a medical call. They had a professional relationship now, and it would be smart for her to remember that.

"Yes. Sorry. I probably shouldn't have used my paperwork for personal reasons, but I'm hoping you'll forgive me. I was actually wondering if you were busy tonight."

Cynthia took in a deep breath and tried to organize her thoughts. He was okay—that was the first big relief—but he was asking her out? She tried to keep her tone light and professional. "It's me and a couple of episodes of streamed TV tonight."

"Is that what you want to do?"

She could hear the cajoling smile in his voice. She should say no to whatever it was he was going to propose. Except she was getting mighty tired of lonely Friday nights. She'd moved here and jumped right in at work. Sure, she'd found a church, but plugging in was a bigger challenge. The area was a transient one—so many people in DC were here for a short time because of government or military assignments. Cynthia didn't want to find herself in a long-distance relationship at this point. And the people who lived here more permanently still gave her the side-eye, probably waiting to see if she'd stick. Plus, she was fifty-five, and no matter how she counted those years, she definitely didn't fall into the spring chicken category any longer.

"That's a long pause. I made things awkward, didn't I?"

"No. You didn't, Joe, I promise. I was thinking."

"It's always been a habit of yours."

Her lips curved. "The truth is, no, it's not what I want to do. I was simply debating the wisdom of doing anything else."

"I'm harmless. You know that."

She snorted. "That isn't one of the adjectives that would ever have come up when I was thinking of you. Even so, what did you have in mind?"

"Dinner and conversation? Maybe some Scrabble? I'm pretty sure I still have a board around somewhere."

Dinner and Scrabble. She caught the little sigh before she could let it go. It sounded perfect. "Where can we eat and then play a game?"

"My place. Is that too forward? I can take you out on the town, if you'd rather, but that does take a game off the table."

She closed her eyes and sank to the side of the bed. She knew a little of what Alice must have felt like when she stood with her arms pinwheeling on the edge of the rabbit hole. It was a terrible idea. She could fill a book with all the reasons she should say no. "Text me your address."

"Let me send a car for you. Then I won't have to worry about you driving home."

Send a car. Like it was the most normal, natural thing. Although to him, it probably was. "When was the last time you drove?"

"The day I ended up in the hospital. I don't always use a driver, but you have to admit it makes sense given the traffic around here. I get a lot done on my trips to and from the office. And it keeps me from getting worked up about congestion. Surely that's a good reason?"

She laughed. "Got me there. This is surreal, Joe. You know that, right?"

"Maybe a little. But probably not for the same reasons. I never thought I'd have the chance to ask you to dinner again, let alone have you consider saying yes."

"There's that. I guess I'll text you my address. I'm in Tyson's."

"Thanks. Be comfortable, would you? I've never understood the people who dress up for dinner."

"I'll keep that in mind." She had no intention of throwing on the leggings and tunic she'd planned to wear for her thrilling Friday night at home. The pantsuit she'd worn to work, minus the blazer, would be fine. It wasn't *un*comfortable.

"Harold should be there in about an hour. Will that work?"

She let her breath out slowly as butterflies danced in her stomach. "Yeah. I'll be ready. If you have him call, I can come down to the lobby so he doesn't have to park."

"Okay. Thanks, Cyn. I'm looking forward to seeing you outside of a doctor's office."

"I'll see you in a bit." She ended the call and bit her lip. For better or worse, she was going to dinner with Joe Robinson. At his home.

She didn't even know where that was. In the DC area, obviously, but where? Was he near Tyson's Corner, like she was? His offices were—she'd seen the bold colored logos across the tops of a cluster of high-rise office buildings when she was driving to work or to the mall. Joe had always been a hard worker, and it appeared to have paid off. He headed an enormous company with multiple arms—and they were all employee owned. How had he managed to avoid the necessity of going public? It was a question all the magazine write-ups asked. He usually dodged the question, choosing instead to focus on the products and employees.

Joe was a billionaire. He didn't live in Tyson's. He was probably over in the shaded mansions of Great Falls or McLean with a view of the Potomac.

Cynthia looked around her bedroom. What would Joe think of her place? She did well for herself, but her couple of millions would look like pocket change to him. Was he still focused on money as a symbol of success? How would he not be?

That was one of the places they'd had to agree to disagree in college. To her, then and now, money was a means to an end. To Joe? It was the ultimate goal.

Was it still?

She traded her heeled shoes from her office work for flat, dressier sandals. At least her feet would be happier.

An hour later, almost to the minute, Joe's driver called from a block away. Cynthia checked her hair, grabbed her purse, and headed to the lobby.

It wasn't a limousine. That was something.

The shiny, black Town Car slid into the pickup area of her building like a panther. The driver stepped out as Cynthia exited the revolving door.

"Dr. Mitchell?"

"That's me. Cynthia, please. May I sit up front?"

The driver's eyebrows shot up, but he smoothly shut the rear door and opened the front instead. "If you wish."

"Thanks. It's Harold, isn't it?"

He gave a slight nod as he closed her door.

Cynthia buckled her seat belt as he rounded the car and settled behind the wheel. "Thank you for coming to get me. I realize it's probably out of the way."

"It's no trouble, ma'am." He shifted into drive and headed back into traffic.

She hid a smile. He wasn't one for conversation, apparently. And he hadn't liked her sitting in the front, but he hadn't objected, which suggested it wasn't completely out of the ordinary. She hadn't been able to see Joe tucked in the back of a car being ferried around. He probably sat up here a lot of the time as well. Unless it suited him to be seen as someone powerful enough to be driven around. That probably had some kind of competitive advantage in certain circumstances.

"Tell me about yourself, Harold."

He jolted and shot a confused glance her way. "Ma'am?"

She sighed. "Doesn't Joe talk to you? I imagine you're a part of his family at this point."

"Yes, ma'am." His voice was full of suspicion.

"Did you know Joe and I knew each other in college?" She wiggled in her seat to get more comfortable. It was an understatement. They'd been inseparable in college, first as friends—nearly instantaneous friends—then more. She'd never had a connection like that with anyone before. Or since.

"No, ma'am."

She grinned. "You're a tough nut, Harold."

She thought she caught his lips twitching. "Yes, ma'am."

This time she laughed. "If you don't want me to make small talk, you could turn on the radio. I promise I won't tell Joe, if that's a worry."

"He's already going to be annoyed you didn't sit in the back." Harold shook his head and reached for the dial in the middle of the dashboard. "Music preferences?"

"Whatever you like will be fine. I listen to doctor's office music most of the day. If I don't like it, I can tune it out."

Harold made a sound that might have been a chuckle. "Joe prefers classic rock."

"He always did. That's fine." It had been a while. The first years after they went their separate ways, Cynthia had avoided memories of their time together, which meant avoiding the music. It had become a habit. She'd developed a taste for indie rock—there were a lot of great girl power anthems and tales of overcoming broken hearts. There were also enough guitars to keep it from sliding into whining. Or country. Which was basically the same thing in her mind.

She looked out the window as they took the ramp onto 66 heading into the city. Where did he live?

"Georgetown, ma'am."

Cynthia glanced over at Harold. She must have spoken the words out loud.

"You didn't know?"

She shook her head. "I thought maybe Great Falls. I know he has the money to live wherever he wants. I don't think I would have pictured in him the city though."

"It was part of a bailout."

"What do you mean?"

Harold cleared his throat and checked the mirrors. "It was in the papers. Local ones, at least. A few years back, the owner of a small video game company approached him to see if Joe wanted to buy him out. There were all sorts of issues and it was either finding a buyer or bankruptcy. I guess they were friends of a sort, so Joe bought the company. Turned out the guy was also completely overextended on his mortgage, so Joe bought the house at enough of a profit to the other guy that he could down-size, relocate, and not end up on the street."

She smiled. That sounded like Joe. "He's always had a generous heart."

"Yes, ma'am. This time, it landed him with eleven thousand square feet from 1840 that he has to deal with."

"Wow."

"Something like that. He always talks about selling and moving into a penthouse somewhere." Harold shrugged as they exited the highway in Rosslyn and worked their way over the Key Bridge. "I don't think he ever will."

Georgetown was on her list of places to explore when she had a free day. Seeing it now, bustling on a Friday evening, was interesting. Would she want to live here? Not that she ever would, but a brief fantasy wasn't unreasonable. She was having dinner with an old flame, nothing more.

It didn't matter that she found him every bit as attractive today as she had before.

It couldn't matter.

It wouldn't matter.

Oh, who was she kidding?

Harold pulled the car over by the curb in front of a bright yellow colonial. It wasn't what she expected at all. From the front it was rather ordinary—other than the color. It didn't look large enough to be what Harold said, either.

He opened her door and offered his hand to help her from the car.

"Thank you, Harold."

"My pleasure, ma'am." He turned and nodded. "Evening, Joe."

She looked up. Joe stood on columned porch that protected the door, hands tucked in the pockets of his jeans, feet bare.

"Hi, Joe."

He smiled and everything in her warmed. Her heart sped up. He stepped down the four steps to the bricked sidewalk and held out his hand. "I'm so glad you came."

5

S he was a vision. He couldn't catch any other thought clearly—everything about Cynthia being here, at his door, flooded over him.

Cynthia studied him for a moment, then nodded and took his hand. "You look good, Joe. Better than you did in the office on Wednesday."

"I don't like doctors' offices."

She laughed. "Who does?"

"Come on in. Mario says dinner's almost ready." He looked past her toward the curb. "Thank you, Harold. Doris asked me to remind you that she's got your supper ready and that she's been practicing, so you shouldn't expect to win tonight."

Harold laughed. "In her dreams."

"Chess?" Cynthia glanced at Harold.

"Xbox. She found a boat racing game she likes."

Joe snickered. "Good luck."

"Are the two of them together?" Cynthia glanced over her shoulder at Harold then back at Joe.

"I don't think so, but I get the feeling Doris might like them to be." Joe shrugged. "Harold will figure it out. They've both got the too-young-for-their-first-names thing going on. Maybe that's enough common ground to start."

Joe pulled the front door closed behind them and looked around the foyer, trying to see what she did. He'd left the décor the way it had been when he moved in. The would-be video game baron had been happy enough not to have to try and sell the furniture separately. They'd taken whatever had mattered to them—and that hadn't seemed to be much. The rugs, chairs, drapes, and art all fit the space. Which gave Joe one less thing to have to worry about. "Do you want a tour?"

"Maybe eventually." She peeked through an archway into the front sitting room and little lines appeared between her eyes. "You mentioned dinner on the phone. I'm starved."

He grinned and relaxed his shoulders. She'd always loved food. "Then let's eat."

He led her through the house, down the hall to the dining room and then into the breakfast room that was attached and had doors that led onto the terrace in back. "I thought we'd eat in here. I don't use the formal dining room . . . I was going to say 'much.' It's probably more accurate to say 'ever.'"

"It's a lovely house. Your designer really kept the colonial feel while making it modern and approachable."

"That was all here. I got the house as part of a business deal —it made more sense for everyone to just buy the stuff inside, too." He shrugged and pulled a chair out from the round glass table. "Why don't you sit? I'll let Mario know we're ready for the food. Do you want a glass of wine or something?"

"I'll have what you're having."

"I don't drink anymore. It's not a problem if you want something, though." Hopefully she wouldn't ask. It wasn't a big story —not really, but he'd just as soon not get into it right now. Was there any way she could look at him now and see the man she used to love? It might be stupid, but Cynthia Mitchell was still everything he was looking for in a woman. Maybe this was a second chance.

"Whatever you're having is fine." She smiled and spread her napkin in her lap.

With a nod, Joe went back into the dining room and into the kitchen.

His chef, Mario, was a bull of a man. He'd been a Marine for twenty years before getting out and going to culinary school. Joe never questioned anything the man said—they might be close to the same age, but Mario terrified him.

"We're ready."

"Good. I don't like my food to get cold. Start with those salads." He nodded to the two plates sitting on the counter. "When you're finished, bring back those plates and I'll have the entrees ready."

"You know, some people would expect me to have serving staff."

Mario snorted. "Shows what some people know. There's already vinaigrette on it, so don't come back in here looking for ranch. You hear me?"

Joe wrinkled his nose as he picked up the plates.

"I saw that."

He chuckled. "Of course you did. Thanks, Mario. I'll be back in a few."

"I need at least ten minutes."

"Got it." Joe carried the salads back and set one in front of Cynthia before taking the seat on her left. "Mario said he already dressed the salad, and we're not to ask for ranch."

She grinned. "He bosses you around?"

"Absolutely." Joe held out his hand. "Can we say grace?"

Her eyebrows lifted, but she twined her fingers through his.

Joe fought the urge to hunch his shoulders at her obvious

surprise. He said a quick blessing over their meal and time together.

Cynthia forked up a bite. "This is lovely."

"That's Mario. He's a genius."

"Well, I approve. And I'm glad there's no ranch in sight. This is much healthier."

He fought the urge to roll his eyes. "Healthy" had become the number one buzzword out of Mario's mouth. "About that."

"Yes?" She picked through her salad.

"You still make everything into the perfect bite, I see."

Her cheeks pinked. "I don't think there's anything wrong with enjoying my food."

"There isn't." Joe stabbed the lettuce and took a bite. "Which brings me back around to the 'healthy' thing. Will there be a time when I can enjoy food again? Or is healthy going to follow me forever?"

Cynthia chuckled. "Healthy can be enjoyable. But a cheat day now and then isn't going to be a problem down the road."

Cheat day. Even the name was stupid. He probably shouldn't say that out loud. But he could tell Mario to work them into the meal plan, because if Joe didn't get something that tasted good soon, he wasn't sure he was going to be able to continue to say staying alive was worth it.

"So, how's work? Have you caught up from your time off?" Her eyes danced with laughter.

"Not really. I was told I should be limiting my hours to nine or ten a day. So I have been. I'll get caught up eventually." Or, he wouldn't, and he'd find out that the people under him were perfectly capable of handling it. They were. He already knew that. It was just tough to leave everything in someone else's hands. "How about you? Had any noncompliant patients this week?"

"Touché. No work talk, then?"

"Probably not. Why don't you instead give me the recap of the last thirty years?"

"Oh, Joe. I gave you and your folks the highlights when we went to lunch after church."

"Sure. Those were the highlights. What about the things you left out?"

Cynthia focused on her salad for several moments.

"Or I can start." Joe set down his fork. He'd gotten through half of his salad, which was more greenery than he usually managed in a week. He'd call it a win. Surely not cleaning his plate was a good thing, too.

She looked up at him, then down at his plate. "You need to finish your salad."

He wrinkled his nose but forked up another bite. "The cloud-based business applications company was my first. They're still the bread and butter, if you look at the whole thing from the top down. Government services, which basically grew out of the business apps and then exploded into its own monster of consulting services, is the next in line. Computer security grew from that and, again, took on a life of its own. They're still fairly intertwined—the government has a lot of computer security needs."

Cynthia laughed. "I imagine they do."

"We work with other people, too. But a lot is on a government contract. Often times as a sub to our own government services arm, but not always."

"Seriously? Why wouldn't you keep it all in-house?"

He grinned and pointed his fork at her. "You've always had a good head for business. We try. Sometimes the contract is only up for a re-bid as a sort of check-the-block activity for the government. They don't want new blood. They're happy with the current contract holder, but regulations and contract length require it. It's better for the business, long term, if we play nice and don't try to be the bully who takes over the sandbox."

She nodded. "No wonder you're busy."

"That's only three of the five. We also have a video game company and our social media platform. They're much more separate. I didn't start them—they were purchases."

"Did you intend to buy them?"

"Harold told you about the house." Joe shook his head and set his fork down. He'd managed close to three-quarters of the salad. Surely that was enough. "I wouldn't have done it if it didn't make good sense. But no, I wasn't looking for either of them. It was a way to help some friends out of a bind."

She reached over and covered his hand. "I think it's sweet. And it's one of the things I'm glad to know hasn't changed. You've always been generous."

His chest swelled. Joe flipped his hand over and squeezed her fingers. "Are you finished with your salad?"

Cynthia glanced down at her empty plate and nodded.

"Great. I'll take these in and see if Mario's got the entrees ready." He stood and slid his plate on top of hers, then balanced their dirty forks on top.

"Joe?"

He turned in the doorway. "Yeah?"

"Why don't you have someone doing that for you?"

He shrugged. The last thing he needed—or wanted—was a whole bunch of staff running around the house. "Mario's busy cooking. It's Doris' night off—though she did offer. And Harold? He sticks his fingers in the food."

Cynthia's laugh followed him out of the room into the kitchen.

❧

CYNTHIA TUCKED her feet under her on the overstuffed chair and watched Joe flip on the electric fire. Her belly was full of good food and nerves. Being with Joe was so natural, so comfortable; it was as if the last thirty years had never happened.

"You're sure you don't want an after-dinner drink?" Joe settled into the chair across the small gaming table from her.

Their knees weren't touching, but she could feel the heat of his body. Or, at least, she imagined she could. "I'm fine, but thank you. I don't drink often enough for it to bother me that you don't at all. To be honest, I'm a hold-a-glass-of-wine-for-several-hours-at-work-related-cocktail-parties-or-fundraisers-and-forget-to-drink-it kind of girl."

He chuckled. "It's always good to have a prop."

"It can be, yes. And I find if I get my own drink, I don't have as many people asking if they can buy me one."

"Still breaking hearts everywhere you go." His voice was a murmur.

Was she supposed to have heard it? Probably not. And yet. "Not everywhere."

His eyebrows lifted. "Oh? Some of them you let stay intact?"

She reached over and swatted his arm. "Joe. If you want the truth, I never met anyone who made it seem like the hassle of navigating a relationship would be worth it."

"I can understand that." He offered a tight smile before opening the Scrabble box he'd placed on the table when he sat. "Do I need to go get the dictionary? I seem to recall you like to use a lot of made-up words."

"They weren't made up. They're medical terms and they're great for triple word scores." She rubbed her hands together. She hadn't played Scrabble in years. There had been a little group of people in med school who'd get together for a game now and then. It faded away before too long—they were all always so busy—but since then? She wasn't one to try and plug into the women's ministries in church. She'd tried at first, but a single woman who was a doctor had nothing in common with a young mom of three under three.

Maybe that was unfair. Just like the tiny wisp of envy—or was it regret?—was unfair. Cynthia liked her life. It was a good life. More than that, she was absolutely certain it was the life God wanted her to be living.

But it didn't mean that every now and then she didn't wish for what could have been.

"Draw a tile, and let's see who goes first." Joe offered the cloth bag of wooden tiles.

Cynthia reached in and drew out an "A."

"Ha."

"I could still get a blank tile." Joe grinned and reached in. He flipped the tile over and frowned. "'B.' It's always 'B.'"

She laughed along with him and dropped her "A" tile back in the bag before reaching in and rummaging around to pull out her seven starting tiles and arranging them on the little wooden stand.

Joe grabbed his tiles and nodded. "All right, Cyn, show me what you've got."

Cynthia arranged her tiles on the starting space.

"Gherkin? You seriously drew—" Joe broke off and blew out a breath. "Unbelievable."

"Sorry if that puts you in a pickle."

He groaned. "You did not just do that."

She grinned and replaced her tiles. "Your turn."

"Like I'm going to be able to beat 'gherkin.'" Joe frowned.

The clock on the mantle ticked into the silence. Cynthia settled back and considered her new letters. There were options. It would depend on what Joe did. The easiest, of course, would be to add an "S" to her opening word. If he had one. That would give him a triple word score. She almost hadn't played the whole word because it set him up to piggyback off her. But in college, Joe usually missed those sorts of easy point grabs. He said it wasn't sporting.

She figured points were points.

"Maybe before we both die of old age?" Cynthia shifted in her seat.

"Yeah, yeah." Joe dropped an "O" and a "D" under her "G." "Happy?"

"Very." She added his points to the notepad and cleared her throat before setting an "S" at the end of "gherkin."

Joe groaned. "Remind me why we play this game? You always do that."

"That's exactly why we play it. I like to win."

"Is that why you're such a good surgeon? I've been reading up on you. You've got an impressive résumé these days. You've come a long way from being the scrappy and determined pre-med student I knew."

She considered his words as he played some tiles. The compliment warmed her, but was there a hidden barb as well? Was she not supposed to have been successful, too? "It's part of it, I guess. I don't see it just as winning—it's helping people stick around to be available for their families. And at the end of the day, if God has determined it's someone's time to go, nothing I do is going to make a difference. I know that. Unlike some of my compatriots, I realize there's a difference between being a doctor and being God."

He smiled. "You've always been grounded and sure of your faith."

"Not always. Everyone doubts at some point or another." She tilted her head to the side and studied him. Joe had aged well. He wore the air of a powerful man easily but, at the same time, managed to remain approachable. "Did you lose your faith?"

Joe sighed and drew replacement tiles. "Maybe not lost.

Misplaced it for a while, I guess. It's not easy to work hard for something and not take credit for your success. At least, it wasn't for me."

"And now?" Cynthia set out her tiles, joining one of his words to make a new one. Maybe she shouldn't push, but this mattered. In college, they'd shared a basic faith. It had always felt like it mattered more to her, but it wasn't as if Joe wasn't a believer.

"I'm remembering. Apparently, heart surgery makes you think."

She laughed. "I've heard that."

"I'm grateful you were there. Have I thanked you for taking care of me in the operating room?" He looked up and their eyes met.

Cynthia struggled to breathe. His gaze had always been potent. Why could he draw her in so easily? She'd prayed for God to bring him back to her all through medical school. She'd kept an obsessive eye on the business news, tracking his successes, thinking that surely he'd hit a point where he'd realize the two of them could make it work. He never had. All those unanswered prayers. Well, answered in a way she hadn't wanted.

She looked down at the letters in front of her, breaking his gaze. What if God's answer hadn't been "no"? What if He'd been saying "wait"?

6

"Knock, knock."

Joe glanced up from his monitor. "Hey, Ty. Come on in."

Tyler Shaw, Chief Technology Officer and essentially Joe's right-hand man when it came to all things corporate, shut the door behind himself and sank into one of the visitor chairs. He was young for his position, but he handled it well. And Joe had only ever cared that he had the right people in the right roles. Age was just a number.

When Tyler didn't speak, Joe did. "What's up?"

"You haven't heard."

Joe's eyebrows lifted and he sorted through the mental list of business deals and contracts that were in the pipe, coming up blank when he tried to put a finger on a problem. He shook his head. "Apparently not. Tell me."

"It's Danielle. She..." Tyler paused and cleared his throat. "She was in a bad accident on her way in this morning."

"Why aren't you at the hospital? You should go. We can handle things here."

"I—thanks. I'll go soon. Her parents are there, and they told me not to rush." Tyler rubbed the back of his neck. "She's still in surgery. There's a lot of swelling on her brain. Pressure. Internal bleeding. I don't—she might not—"

"I'm calling Harold. He'll meet you at the front and take you to the hospital. Do you know where to go when you get there?" Joe definitely didn't want Tyler driving. The man looked lost. Shattered. "Didn't you propose this weekend?"

Tyler winced. "I put it off one more week. She was so busy, on deadline. Now she might not get the chance . . ."

"Don't think like that. You can't. You need to hold on to hope." Joe stood and moved around his desk to perch on the edge. Tyler went to church—they'd had a few conversations about God here and there, though neither of them had pushed the other for deeper explanations. "Can we pray?"

Tyler jolted and looked up like a drowning man seeking help. "You'd do that?"

"Of course." Joe bit his lower lip. He'd offered, and he would follow through. Even if it was like exercising a muscle that hadn't been used in decades. He'd been doing more praying since waking up in the hospital. It helped that his mother kept texting him, asking what he was reading in the Bible each day, what prayer requests he could share with her. They'd done that in college—both of his parents. After graduation, he'd stopped responding. Gradually, they'd stopped trying. It was good to have it back. He needed the encouragement.

He closed his eyes and, after a brief hesitation, put his hand on Tyler's shoulder. "Dear Jesus, we're coming to You right now to ask Your mercy and grace on Danielle. Strengthen and heal her body. Give the doctors wisdom and skill. And above all else, comfort Tyler and her parents—all the people who love Danielle. She's an amazing young woman who loves you. Amen."

Tyler reached up and briefly covered Joe's hand. "Thanks, Joe."

"Keep me posted? And let her parents know that we're praying for Danielle." Joe stood and slipped his phone from his pocket. "By the time you get downstairs, Harold should be pulling around. If you need anything—if there's anything I can do—just say the word. I mean it."

"I appreciate it." Tyler stuffed his hands in his pockets. "What if she doesn't make it?"

Joe closed his eyes. It wasn't good to think that way, but it was so hard not to. "We'll figure it out. For now, you need to go be there so when she's out of surgery, you can see her. You both need that."

"Okay." Tyler nodded and scrubbed his hands over his face. "You're right. Thanks, Joe."

"Go." Joe patted Tyler's shoulder and nudged him toward the door before thumbing open a text to Harold. He gave a short explanation—enough to get Harold in the car and moving—Joe could always provide more detail if needed. Realistically, Harold would pump Tyler for whatever details there were, and he'd be the one filling Joe in later.

Joe sat back down at his desk and studied the report he'd been reading when Tyler came in. He couldn't focus. Was there more he could do?

He drummed his fingers on the desktop. After another minute ticked by, he tapped out a second text to Harold. Depending on the answer, there might be one more thing he could do. There were several good hospitals in the area—there was no guarantee they'd taken Danielle to the same hospital Cynthia worked at. But there was a chance. And if they had? Maybe she could help somehow.

It was always worth asking.

His phone buzzed and he grinned. Joe could always count on

Harold. And in this case, it looked like he had one more string to pull.

Joe opened his contacts and scrolled to Cynthia's entry. Office? No, they were past that. Weren't they? He tapped her personal cell and swiveled to look out the window over the Tyson's Corner area while it rang.

"Dr. Mitchell."

"Hi, Cyn. It's Joe. Do you have a minute?"

The sounds of a busy hospital filled the line—a fuzzy voice over the PA system, squeaks of rubber-soled shoes on tile, and chattering voices. "Sure. Give me one second to step back into my office and shut the door."

He waited and the sounds muted, but didn't disappear completely.

"That's better. How are you?"

"I'm fine. Feeling great, actually." He forced himself to slow down. He didn't want her to think he'd only called for a favor. Except, of course, he had. And he hadn't called since their dinner last Friday. Almost a week ago. He winced. They'd texted a few times, but he should have called. "How are you?"

"Oh, you know. Busy. A little confused."

"Yeah. Sorry. I should have called. I thought about calling." Then he'd talked himself out of it. He didn't want to appear too eager—which was stupid. This wasn't college any more. "I don't really have an excuse. Forgive me?"

She hummed quietly. "This time. I actually hoped I'd see you on Sunday."

Joe fought the urge to hunch his shoulders. He'd meant to go to church, too. "If it helps, my mom already scolded me well enough and I can promise it won't happen again."

Cynthia laughed. "Your mom knows her way around a scold. All right. I'll let it pass, too. I'm glad you called today. I don't have a lot of time right now, but I'd love to see you again."

"I'd like that, too. What time do you get off work? I could pick you up and we could grab a bite to eat." There was work he'd planned to do tonight—directly against all orders to start cutting back on his hours—but it could be set aside if it meant he had some time with Cyn.

"Six? But I can meet you somewhere. You don't need to come back out this way after you've gone home."

"I actually need to swing by the hospital later, anyway." He cleared his throat. "It's one of the reasons I called."

"Oh?" Curiosity mixed with a hint of disappointment in her tone.

"One of my employees—the almost-fiancée of my CTO—was admitted after a bad traffic accident this morning."

"Oh. Yes, I heard the pages for that. Six cars. She was one of them?"

"Apparently. Tyler—that's my CTO—didn't have a lot of details. Just that she was in surgery and that there was a lot of pressure and bleeding in her skull."

"Mmm. The life flight."

His stomach dropped. Had Danielle been airlifted? That wasn't something Tyler mentioned. Had he known? "I don't know."

"I do. Doctors talk. I had a brief consult as they were worried about her heart briefly. I'll be honest, Joe, she's in bad shape."

He blew out a breath. It wasn't what he wanted to hear. "Tyler's headed over there—might even be there by now, honestly. I sent him with Harold. Is there any way you could get the scoop and fill him in?"

"Her doctors will let the family know. Does she have family locally?"

"Her parents are there."

"And they're friendly with Tyler? They're okay with him being there?"

"Oh, yes. Absolutely. They consider him a son already as far as I know."

"I'll have to talk to them. I can't just go around giving out medical information. And the reality is, her doctors might not want to share with me. We usually know other doctors only show up to ask questions when it's a friend of the family type of situation. But I'll see what I can do. No promises."

"That's great. I appreciate anything you can do. Even if it's just to stop by and say hello to Tyler and let him know I'll be swinging by."

"Do you still want to grab dinner?"

"I do. Even if you'd said you wouldn't do anything, not even go say hi, I would still want to have dinner with you tonight. They're separate. Completely separate."

"Okay. If you're sure."

"I'm sure."

"Then I'll head over to the surgical waiting area when I'm finished here and look for you."

"That should work. If we end up somewhere else, I'll text you. Thanks, Cyn. Seriously." Joe ended the call and stared out over the bustling streets below. He'd bungled things. That wasn't what he wanted, at all.

He wanted . . . well, he wanted to get things back to where they'd been all those years ago.

Was it possible?

Maybe he'd add that to the list of things his mom could pray for.

Cynthia made her way back out to the waiting area. She'd found a few minutes to head over and introduce herself to Tyler. He was a sweet kid—she saw why Joe was so involved. In so many ways, Tyler was a carbon copy of Joe when she'd first known him. Danielle's parents seemed to appreciate having him there with them—though they also had seemed surprised that he was. Was Tyler already headed down the path Joe had taken? The one where work was the sum total of his life?

Not that she could really say much about that. She'd done the same thing. Just not quite to the same degree as Joe. She hadn't stopped going to church. She still had friends whom she saw socially. Work wasn't the only thing she did.

She gave herself a firm mental shake to stop her wandering thoughts as she crossed to where the three of them huddled.

"What did they say?" Danielle's mother jumped to her feet and reached for Cynthia's hands, clinging to them as if they were her only lifeline.

"They've got probably another two hours of work to do. The surgeon is one of the best." Cynthia didn't know him personally, but she'd heard his name, and the nurses spoke well of him. This hospital didn't hire anyone who wasn't close to the top of their field. "I didn't speak to him, directly. You can imagine he's busy, but I did speak to one of the surgical assistants. Right now, they're cautiously optimistic."

"She'll be okay?" Danielle's mother's eyes filled.

"No one can promise anything." Cynthia eased her hands out of the woman's grasp and gently rubbed her arm. "But it's going as well as it possibly can."

Tyler's Adam's apple bobbed as he swallowed. Danielle's parents wrapped each other into an embrace, leaving him standing on the outside of comfort. Cynthia frowned and stepped closer to him. "How are you doing?"

He shook his head.

She smiled slightly. It was an honest response. She hated being on this side of the waiting room doors. She hated being the one to bring inconsequential news to waiting family, too.

"Joe said he'd be here when he finished at work to check on you."

"Joe's coming here?" Confusion clouded Tyler's eyes. "Are you sure she's going to make it?"

"Yes. Is it really so unusual for Joe to do something like that?"

"No. I mean I guess not. Just usually you can't pry him out of the office before nine. And even then, he takes work home with him. He's really coming here when he's finished?"

"He really is. He told me around six."

"Six? Tonight at six?" Tyler gave a short, disbelieving laugh. "I guess we'll see."

Cynthia frowned. "Has he been going home around supper-time every day since his attack?"

"Maybe, if supper is at nine."

"And when does he get in? In the morning?"

Tyler shrugged. "He's always there before me. I generally get in at eight thirty. Most of my immediate team starts their day at nine, so I like to get a little head start. Why?"

"Nothing." Her voice was a murmur. It wasn't anything for Tyler to worry about, but it was definitely something she'd be taking up with Joe. He'd agreed to her restrictions. He needed to abide by his word. She checked the time. "I really do need to get back to my own work. Will you be okay?"

"Yes. Of course. Thank you for this. I realize it may not seem like you did much, but you did. Waiting is easier when you have a little glimmer of hope to hold onto." Tyler offered his hand.

Cynthia didn't bother stopping her reflex and pulled the young man into a hug. She stepped back and smiled. "I'll be praying for Danielle. And for you."

"Thanks." He glanced at Danielle's parents who were still wrapped in each other's arms. "I'll let them know."

She gave a short nod and turned, slipping her phone out of her pocket as she strode through the halls back toward cardiology. Thankfully there was nothing urgent to handle this afternoon.

What was going on with Joe? They'd had a lovely time on Friday night. Or she'd thought so, at least. He'd given every indication that he agreed. It was just like old times. There was no awkwardness. No long gaps of silence where neither one of them knew what to say. Just the quiet, comfortable conversation that they'd always been able to share.

It had warmed her. Filled her.

Given her hope.

She shut her office door and leaned against it, letting her eyes close. So much hope. And maybe it was premature.

Everything about Joe drew her in, just like it always had. He was attractive—although that had a lot less pull than it used to. She'd met a lot of good-looking men in the last thirty years. So few of them had the kind of soul-deep goodness that Joe did.

And maybe her parents were right. She'd used Joe as a yardstick for everyone she'd dated. They'd all fallen short. And now? Was Joe going to miss the mark, too, because he simply wasn't the ideal she'd created in her head?

She wanted this to work. Being with Joe made it seem like everything in her life was finally where it was supposed to be.

What was she supposed to do?

7

J oe scanned the waiting room before crossing to where Tyler slumped in a chair. He was a little distance from Danielle's parents. Joe filed that away. There could be any number of benign reasons for that. But it could also be a bad sign. He sat in the empty seat beside Tyler and cleared his throat.

Tyler shifted and opened an eye, then straightened. "Joe. You came."

"Didn't Cynthia tell you I would?"

"Sure." Tyler glanced at his watch. "I just didn't believe her. It's not even half past five."

"You're more important to me than paperwork. You know that, don't you?"

Tyler shrugged.

Great. That was not a rousing agreement. "Well, you are. And I'm sorry if I haven't made that clear before now."

"Okay. Thanks."

"So how is she?"

"Still in recovery, last I heard. They said something about needing her room to be ready before they could move her. We can't see her until she's there—and I'm worried that they'll take so long that it'll be family only."

"But surely—"

Tyler shook his head. "Her parents made it clear that I'm not family."

"That's new." Joe cocked his head to the side. "Any idea why?"

"Nope. They know I'm planning to propose this weekend. Or, well, I was planning to. I guess that's on hold now."

"Why? You can still propose. Maybe it won't be exactly the same." Joe broke off as Tyler shook his head.

"No way. I have to wait now. She wouldn't want a hospital proposal. I had it all planned out, with a photographer and everything." He winced and slipped his phone out of his pocket. "I should cancel her. I wonder how much that's going to cost."

Joe reached out to touch Tyler's arm. "Postpone it. Explain the situation and say you're going to wait a week or two for her to get back on her feet."

"Don't you get it? It's not going to be a week or two. It can't possibly be that fast. They don't do five hours of surgery when you're going to bounce back like it's nothing." Tyler turned away, his shoulders stiff.

"Hey. God's got this."

Tyler snorted.

"What? Am I wrong?"

"No." He sighed and turned back to Joe. "But it's weird to hear something like that coming from you. You're really embracing this now, aren't you?"

Guilt swamped him. He was embracing his faith— near-death experiences would, apparently, cause that—but he should have been doing that all along. "My faith isn't new. I haven't been where I should have been. I've let a lot slide. I'm sorry it got bad enough that this is so startling for you. I should have been a better example."

Tyler shrugged. "In some ways, it's nice to know you're not perfect."

Joe laughed. "I'm absolutely not. But I am here for you. And for Danielle."

"Thanks. Do you want to meet her parents?"

Joe nodded.

"Come on." Tyler tucked his phone back in his pocket and led the way across the waiting area to Danielle's parents. "Mr. and Mrs. Hicks?"

"Tyler, honey, you should go home."

Tyler's gaze flicked over to Joe then back to Mrs. Hicks. "I'd like to wait and see her settled in a room. Maybe find out what the doctor has to say."

"Oh, now, son, we can call you tomorrow and give you the scoop. Or you can come by after work tomorrow evening." Mr. Hicks shook his head. "There's no point in everyone's life being disrupted like this."

"I'd really like to stay. I—you know I planned to propose to Danielle this weekend. She's my world." Tyler blinked rapidly and cleared his throat. "I wanted to introduce our boss—well, the CEO of the company, so he's everyone's boss—but anyway, this is Joe."

Joe smiled and held out his hand. "Joseph Robinson. Everyone calls me Joe. I wish we'd been able to meet under better circumstances. Danielle is a highly valued member of our team. I'm praying for her to have a quick recovery."

Mrs. Hicks' hand was cool and limp for the three seconds it was in his.

Mr. Hicks' grip was a vise of iron that held on too long. "You're a praying man?"

"Yes, sir." Joe eased his fingers out of the handshake and fought the urge to shake them.

Mr. Hicks nodded once and pinned Tyler with narrowed eyes. "You can stay. You understand that our daughter is our priority right now, not your plans for romance."

Tyler nodded.

Joe thought he could see Mr. Hicks' arrows hitting their mark in Tyler's psyche. Poor kid. "If I had a daughter, I can't think of anyone I'd rather see her in love with than Tyler. He's a good man. I'm proud to know him."

Mrs. Hicks shifted and stared balefully at Joe. "If you had children, you'd understand how hard it is to let them go."

"I imagine it is. But then, I also hope I'd be able to say I did my best to provide them with a strong foundation for their adult lives, so I could trust them to be the adults God made them to be." Joe smiled to soften his words.

"You beat me. I thought I'd end up having to wait." Cynthia slid her arm through Joe's and smiled cheerily at the group. "I just finished checking with one of the nurses on Danielle's floor. They should be sending someone for you soon."

"That's good news." Mr. Hicks rubbed his wife's arm before repeating himself, as if to ensure that he believed it. "That's good. We appreciate your help, Dr. Mitchell."

"It's my pleasure. I'm just grateful Joe called and asked if there was anything I could do to get the information flowing a little more freely. You've had a long, trying day. I know you're going to object, but hear me out. Once you've gotten to see Danielle, please go home. Get some dinner. Take a shower. Step away for a few hours. Sleep, if you can. She's going to need you at your best." Cynthia's voice was gentle but firm.

"Oh, I don't think—"

Mr. Hicks cut his wife off. "Thank you for your concern. We were just trying to tell Tyler he should go on home, too."

"After I see Danielle." A thin thread of steel ran through Tyler's words.

Joe smothered a smile. That was the tone Tyler used in the boardroom, and it usually meant he got his way. "Please let Danielle know we're praying for her, and she shouldn't worry about anything at work. We'll be looking forward to her return when she's healthy."

Cynthia tugged on his arm.

Joe took the hint. It was time to go. When they'd gone down the hall a ways, he glanced back over his shoulder. Tyler had returned to his corner on the opposite room from Danielle's parents. He shook his head. That didn't bode well.

"What?" Cynthia glanced back then shot a confused look at Joe.

"They're trying to shut him out. He was going to propose this weekend, and now they're trying to send him home without seeing her. I don't like it. He's a good kid."

"Calm down, Papa Bear." Cynthia chuckled. "It's been a hard day for everyone. I'm sure they're just reacting to the stress. Circle the wagons, you know? Your parents did that."

"What do you mean?"

"Didn't you think it was odd that no one from your office visited you in the hospital?"

He had. And he hadn't. He was the company owner. "I imagined everyone would think it was weird. They called and emailed."

"Several tried to come by. Your mom shooed them away."

"Of course she did." He sighed. It was a hopeful sign. Maybe. "I guess that's what moms do?"

She nodded. "Now. If you can, let's set that aside. Where are you taking me for dinner?"

Joe laughed. "Didn't I ask you to choose?"

"I don't recall that."

Which didn't mean he hadn't asked. He mentally scanned through the restaurants in the area, finally landing on a little mom-and-pop steakhouse not too far away. "All right. No criticizing my choice then."

She drew an X over her heart like she'd always done in college, and he melted. Why had he ever let her get away?

CYNTHIA CLICKED her phone to check the screen, then clicked it back off. Where was Joe? They'd had a lovely dinner out on Wednesday night—although he'd used the opportunity to sneak off his suggested diet.

She smiled in spite of herself. He was like a little kid getting caught stealing candy. It was hard to stay mad at him. And he promised that Mario was keeping him on the straight and narrow at home. Including packed lunches for the office.

A treat now and then wasn't a bad thing. Probably.

He'd sent Harold and his car for her again on Friday night and they'd cozied up with the Scrabble board in front of the fire after a lovely meal.

It was just like old times, if she could move past the enormous Georgetown mansion, complete with housekeeper, chef, and driver. She'd gotten to meet Doris this time. She wasn't the matronly woman of Cynthia's imagination. She was probably in her thirties, like Harold. And Joe said he thought the two of them were working their way toward love.

Joe would probably know. He'd always been able to tell in college.

Was that why he'd ended things between them? Had he known, with whatever foresight he had, that things weren't going to work out?

Was it different now?

The worship band stepped onto the stage. Cynthia frowned. Still no Joe. And no text or call, either. She blew out a breath and tried to put it away. She'd focus on Jesus. He never let her down.

Halfway through the first verse of the first song, someone jostled her elbow. Cynthia glanced over and couldn't stop the grin.

"I'm sorry." Joe whispered in her ear. "I was going to text, then I figured I was almost here so there was no point. I should have gone ahead and done it though, right?"

"It would have been nice, but don't worry about it." Cynthia turned back to the front and started to sing. Her heart lifted when Joe joined in. It was familiar. Comfortable. And yet still new and exciting all over again. She glanced at him from the side of her eye and her insides turned to mush.

Could it work between them now?

She breathed out a prayer for guidance. Loving Joe was something she'd been doing for most of her life. Were they finally at the place where they could do something about it?

When they sat and Pastor Brown invited them to pray, Joe took her hand.

Cynthia's breath caught. Slowly she wove her fingers through his.

At least he was thinking along the same lines as she was.

The service was a blur. Cynthia was hyperaware of her fingers interlaced with Joe's, the gentle pressure of his leg next to hers in the always-a-little-too-close seating, and the rapid thrumming of her heart. She'd scribbled down the sermon passage—she'd have to read it later and stream the replay online.

When the music switched to recorded Christian pop, she looked over at Joe. "What held you up?"

"Tyler called. Danielle's parents have removed him from the visitor list. They're taking turns being at her bedside, so he can't even try to sneak in when she's alone. It's breaking his heart."

She furrowed her brow as she turned to collect her purse and Bible. "They won't say why?"

"Not to him." Joe shrugged. "He needed to vent more than anything. I didn't want to hurry him along or cut him off, so it put me behind. I'm sorry I didn't let you know."

"Don't be. I can't always promise I'll be the best about it, either. Doctors get called at all hours—whether we're on call or not." She debated with herself a moment before adding, "Would you like to come to my place for lunch?"

His eyebrows lifted. "Really?"

She nodded. It was a step she didn't usually take. But this was Joe.

"I'd like that." He cocked his head to the side. "I don't imagine you want to leave your car here?"

Cynthia laughed. "Not particularly."

"Can I ride with you? I could send Harold on his way."

"Of course. Where's Harold waiting? And he knows he can come in, right? Even sit with us, if he wants."

Joe chuckled. "I made that same offer. He said maybe next week."

Fair enough. She wasn't sure what sort of relationship Joe had with his household staff—and wasn't that a hilarious concept?—but it seemed friendly. Joe had never been one for standing on ceremony. She was glad that hadn't changed.

"Hey, Harold."

Harold shifted from where he leaned against Joe's car. "Boss. Ma'am."

"I thought I told you to call me Cynthia."

"Yes, ma'am." Humor sparkled in Harold's eyes.

She shook her head. Obviously he was used to joking around with Joe.

"I'm going to Cyn's for lunch. I'll call you later to arrange picking me up, if that's okay? I'm sorry. If I'd thought it through, we would have planned this so you didn't have to wait through the service."

"It's no problem."

"You can always join us inside." Cynthia lifted an eyebrow. "I'd enjoy knowing you weren't bored out here."

"I wasn't bored, but I appreciate the thought. I'll plan on it next week. I do attend services, just usually on Saturday night. In case you were worried I was a heathen."

Cynthia laughed.

Joe shook his head. "Never a worry about that, Harold. Although, I guess Cyn doesn't know how you've nagged me for years to be better about attending church in person."

"I didn't know that." She cast an appraising glance at the young man and nodded in appreciation. "But I'm glad he has more than his parents reminding him of what's right."

"Yes, ma'am."

"Will you ever call me Cynthia?"

Harold lifted a shoulder before focusing on Joe. "Just let me know when you need me to come get you."

"I can take you home, Joe. There's no need for Harold to be waiting around, even if he's at home doing it."

"I don't want to put you out." Joe frowned.

"You aren't. I offered. Go home, Harold. Enjoy your day. I'll make sure he gets home."

Harold looked between the two of them before nodding once. "You know how to get me if you change your mind. It was nice to see you again, Cynthia."

She grinned.

"He likes you." Joe watched Harold drive away before turning to face her.

They were closer than she'd realized. She drew in a quick, startled breath.

"So do I." His breath was warm and faintly minty on her face.

Her lips curved. "Joe."

He closed the distance between them and his lips were on hers, warm and firm. His arms slid around her waist, leaving a trail of heat. Cynthia sighed as her eyes drifted closed and she melted into the familiar embrace.

8

J oe looked around Cynthia's condo with interest. "Nice digs."

She chuckled as she kicked her shoes into the hall closet and padded toward the kitchen. "Not what you would have imagined for me though, right?"

He strode to the wall of windows that looked out over Tyson's Corner. The sidewalks were busy with people heading to shopping or lunch, and the streets were, as ever, full of cars. Thankfully, the soundproofing was first class. "Not really. I pictured you more as the two-story-brick-Colonial-in-a-neighborhood-with-young-families gal."

"I did that. When I was younger and could fit in with those young families. It never seemed to work. Why was this single woman moving in on their turf? The harder I tried to fit in, the more awkward it became." She shrugged. "So I adjusted. I don't mind condos so much. And the lack of yard work is a bonus."

"You always talked about wanting a big garden. You were going to grow all your own vegetables." Joe angled so he could study her balcony. There weren't any pots out there. He turned to look at her. "What happened to that?"

"Ugh." She made a *yucky* face before turning to the fridge and starting to pull out food. "Do you have any idea how much work that is? I tried. The first year in my first home I had such grand plans. Suffice to say I fed a lot of bugs that summer and got very little for myself. What the bugs didn't eat either never grew, shriveled up from dehydration, or rotted before it even got ripe. Apparently, I'm not a gardener."

Joe chuckled and crossed the living space to sit at the island. "Can I help with anything? I'm good at chopping."

"I've got it. You just sit there and talk. Have you gardened?"

"Oh, no. No. You forget, my mom loves to garden. I already knew how much work that would be."

"Why didn't you say something?"

He shrugged. He could still remember how her face would light up when she discussed her plans for all the fresh veggies she was going to indulge in over the summer. She'd even researched canning so she could stock the pantry with her homegrown delights. He wouldn't have dimmed that light for the world. "I figured you needed to give it a go. Maybe you'd decide you loved it."

She wrinkled her nose as she set a pan on the burner and turned on the burner. "I should probably say thank you, but I don't want to. I spent hours out in the heat trying to get that garden to grow. Dirt under my fingernails that I had to spend extra time scrubbing out, and I still never felt like I got it all."

"You should wear gloves."

"I was!" Cynthia laughed and shook her head as she started deftly chopping veggies into thin strips. "No, gardening is not for me. I'll leave it to the men and women who farm and gratefully pay more than I should at the grocery store for the fruits of their bounty."

Joe reached across and snagged a slice of red bell pepper.

"Does Mario ever let you cook?" She added a splash of oil

then slid the contents of her cutting board into a pan. They hit with a sizzle. She gave the pan a little shake and adjusted the knob on the stove before returning to the board to slice what looked like pre-cooked chicken breasts.

"I dabble. Under his strict supervision. It's more because I want to be self-sufficient when he's on vacation than anything else. And I think it gives him a thrill to teach the boss something new. But I'll never hold a candle to what he can make. Still, I didn't starve the ten years I was fending for myself before Mario." Mostly he owed that to takeout, delivery, and dinner meetings, but Cynthia didn't need to know that.

She nodded.

"So you buy cooked chicken?"

"No." She laughed and slid the chicken into the pan before giving it all a stir. "I buy the family packages, though. It's cheaper per pound and old habits die hard. So I poach them as soon as I get home. Then I can stick some in the freezer and pull them out when I need them. It makes cooking after long, busy days a lot less hassle."

"Smart." He watched her finish and plate the stir fry. Everything she did was in competent, economical movements.

They hadn't talked about their kiss in the church parking lot. He'd eased back when he'd remembered where they were. She'd cleared her throat and pointed to her car. They'd filled the drive with chatter about Tyler, Danielle, and anything other than that kiss.

But oh, that kiss.

"You all right?" Cynthia slid a plate in front of him, set another beside him, and rummaged in one of the kitchen drawers. "You disappeared."

"Just thinking." He breathed in the mix of spicy, fresh scents. "This smells amazing."

"Doctor approved, too." She winked before offering him

silverware and a bottle of sparkling water. "Are you going to make me dig around for a penny?"

"A penny? Oh." He chuckled as she slid onto the stool beside him. He took her hand and kissed her knuckles. "Let's pray. I'll tell you while we eat."

She squeezed his hand and closed her eyes.

Joe offered a short prayer of thanks for the food and Cynthia. But his heart poured out words that he didn't say aloud. He asked God to give him courage and wisdom. And he begged God to let things work between them this time.

"So." She squeezed his hand again before pulling hers away and spreading a napkin on her lap. "You were thinking about . . ."

"Kissing you at church."

Her cheeks pinked. "Anything in particular?"

"I'd like to do it again. Not necessarily at church, but I'm not opposed to that location." He worked up a smile even though nerves churned in his stomach. "I've missed you. More than I think I realized until you were back in my life."

Cynthia held his gaze for three excruciating heartbeats before leaning closer and touching her lips to his. One. Two. Three light kisses.

Joe reached up and cupped her face, holding her close as he deepened the kiss. The sensations were a mass of contradictions: exciting and soothing, unsettling, and yet, he'd never felt so right.

Cynthia leaned away, breaking the kiss. She cleared her throat. "We can do that more often. Definitely. But we should probably stay away from too much of it in private spaces. We're not kids, Joe, but I do still try to honor God in my relationships."

He nodded. Honoring God was a priority—a new one for him. Or, well, a renewed one. In college and shortly thereafter, he'd clung to the idea that sex was only for marriage. But when they'd parted ways and his heart was shattered, he hadn't been able to escape the idea that sex might have kept them together. It was easy enough to find people who would tell you that it was a natural outpouring of love. Even friends who'd said they were believers were willing to call the idea of saving sex for marriage antiquated. Or toxic. After all, if God created it, He must want it to be enjoyed.

It was easier and more satisfying to agree and do what he wanted than to step back and analyze the excuses and recognize them for what they were. After a while, it became an expectation, because really wasn't it perfectly natural for two people to enjoy one another?

"I haven't always made that a priority." The back of Joe's neck burned—from shame or embarrassment? Were they different?

She looked down at her plate and seemed to focus intently on cutting a bite of chicken. "I suppose in today's world that's not a surprise. I haven't always been perfect myself. Though I also haven't done a lot of dating. And I'll admit that temptation has been a factor."

"It's part of why I stepped out of that scene, too."

"Do you have children?" She looked up and held his gaze.

He wanted to look away. Desperately. But Cynthia deserved to know it all. "No. But I'm told I would have."

"I SEE." Dread snaked through Cynthia's stomach. It had always been a possibility, of course. She'd followed his career, and even if she'd discounted the speculation and gossip in the write-ups, it wasn't a stretch to realize he'd been living with a different moral code. At least initially.

"I don't know if you *do*." Joe set his fork down and breathed in deeply. "When I was thirty, we had a big birthday party at the company. That was the year I made my first billion and we were all riding high."

"I remember the press." He'd been linked—extensively linked—to a supermodel that year. And for probably another two years after.

He closed his eyes. "I'd started to believe the things they wrote about me. In my mind, I'd made it all happen. It's hard to keep any sort of focus on God when you're the tech industry's next big thing. And I realize that's not an excuse."

"No. It isn't. But it's an explanation."

"I don't remember who introduced me to Jezzrae. She was at the party—anyone who was anyone had received an invitation. And most of them came. She was everything people expected me to be seen with, you know? And I filled that same need for her. She wanted to be taken more seriously in the modeling world—to get a reputation as more than a pretty face."

"Was she?" Cynthia regretted the words as soon as they were out. But she still was desperate to know the answer. Even at more than fifty years old, she couldn't quite stop comparing herself to the ghosts of his past.

He shrugged. "When she wanted something, she knew how to go after it."

"That's not entirely flattering."

"It wasn't meant to be." Joe slid off the stool and stalked to the wall of windows that looked over Tyson's Corner. "After we'd been together a year, she told me she was pregnant. I think she expected me to propose."

It was a reasonable expectation. Joe had never tried to hide his more traditional, conservative upbringing. Even if he was living the life of a tech world celebrity, he was more reserved than many. "You didn't?"

He shook his head and turned to face her. "Thought about it. But by that point, I was starting to feel used. I was suspicious that she had someone else—maybe more than one. So I told her I wanted a paternity test."

"Ouch."

"Basically. She didn't react well. She screamed, threw things, made a huge scene at one of the restaurants downtown. I still don't go there. I'm sure they'd let me in, but it's too mortifying."

"I'm surprised I didn't read about that."

His chuckle held no mirth. "Money can fix some things. Anyway, I held firm. She proposed to me after about two months of going back and forth, but I told her the same thing. I wanted proof it was mine before I was going to tie myself to her."

Tie himself? Cynthia looked at her food and pushed the plate away. Maybe neither of them was eating lunch after all. "So what happened?"

"A week later, she tells me she miscarried. I don't know if she did. I'm haunted by the idea that she probably had an abortion. That would be on my head. Even if the baby wasn't mine, did my response result in its death?" He shook his head and jammed his hands in his pockets. "We drifted apart pretty fast. She finally ended things. And I realized that sex with someone I wouldn't marry was too complicated so I started keeping relationships light. No more than two, maybe three dates. No chance of more. I wasn't going to be the reason another baby had to die."

"Did it occur to you that she might never have been pregnant?" Cynthia crossed to him and lightly touched his arm. As much as her heart ached because of his story, it was as much for the hurt she heard in his voice as anything. They'd been apart a lot of years. It would be stupid to expect that there had never been anyone else.

"The idea flits in and out. But I can't prove it. Any of it. So do I have any children? Not any that are alive. But I can't say more than that." He held her gaze. "I'm so sorry."

"Joe. I'm not the one you need to ask for forgiveness."

He furrowed his brow. "I don't think Jezzrae has any interest in hearing from me."

"Not her, either." Although Cynthia wouldn't say it was a bad idea, there'd been a lot of years under the bridge and maybe it was better to let that rest. "Have you prayed about this? Confessed it? Asked for peace?"

"No." He blew out a breath. "No, I haven't even thought to."

"Maybe you should."

He nodded. "I will. I—does this change what's happening between us?"

"Not really. No." Cynthia slid her arm around his waist and rested her head on his shoulder. "We weren't together then. And we both have done things we regret. We can't change that. But we can start from here and see where God takes us."

His eyes were shining when they met hers. "I love you, Cyn. I always have."

"I love you, too, Joe." It was something she hadn't thought she'd have the chance to tell him again. It felt right. She breathed a prayer of thanks and leaned up to touch her lips to his. They'd have to figure out what the future held for them— but for the first time in a long time, a future felt possible.

9

In the three weeks since he'd shared about Jezzrae and the baby—or at least, the purported baby—Joe and Cynthia had settled into an easy routine. They grabbed dinner after work whenever they could. They did a mix of things—takeout, trying some of the smaller storefront restaurants in the area, or Cynthia would cook. Fridays, when Joe usually worked from home, he'd send Harold to pick her up, Mario would pull out all the stops for something delightful, and they'd spend the evening after dinner in front of the fire. Sometimes they'd play Scrabble. Sometimes chess. Sometimes they'd just talk.

Or kiss.

He liked those nights the best, although they were more difficult.

Cynthia was a vibrant, beautiful woman. She challenged his mind. And they had an easy friendship born of having known each other years before. Even though they'd been out of touch, it was as if those years had disappeared.

"Mr. Joe?"

"Doris? Come on in." Joe saved the spreadsheet he'd been

working on and rolled his chair to the side so he could see his housekeeper better.

"Mr. Tyler's at the door. I put him in the front parlor, but I can bring him up if you want?"

Tyler was here? Joe frowned. "No, that's okay. I'll come down. Would you mind asking Mario if he has cookies stashed away somewhere? And Tyler's a big fan of Coke if we have any on hand. Otherwise iced tea."

"Sure thing." The young woman smiled and slipped away.

Chewing over what could have convinced Tyler to make the drive from their offices in Tyson's into Georgetown on a Friday afternoon, Joe hurried to the front parlor. "Tyler?"

The man stopped pacing and turned to Joe. Devastation was etched into every feature. "Joe."

"What's wrong?" Joe gestured to the settee. "Sit down and tell me. Just say it fast."

"It's Danielle."

Had she died? The last he'd heard, she was supposed to be released from the hospital today. There was still physical therapy in her future, but otherwise . . . "I don't understand. I thought she was going home?"

"She was. Is. She's home. I stopped by to see her—I figured you wouldn't mind if I took off a little early, and you know I'll make up the hours this weekend."

"I'm not worried about your hours, Tyler."

Tyler managed a ghost of a smile. "Her parents have been more and more distant—pushing me off. I figured it was stress, you know? And that things would start sliding back to normal when she got home."

"But?"

Tyler collapsed onto the settee and propped his elbows on his knees. "I took her flowers—all her favorite fall colors jumbled together. She took them and then asked me who they were from."

"Who they were from?"

Tyler nodded. "She thought I was the delivery man. She doesn't know me, Joe. I tried to explain that it was me. Who I was to her. She just got agitated. Her parents told me it was better if I left. How can she not remember me? Everything else is there. It's just me that's missing."

"Oh, Tyler." Movement in the doorway caught his eye and Joe looked over.

Doris bustled in with a tray of cookies and two tall glasses of fizzing soda. She paused in front of Tyler before touching his shoulder. "I heard. I'm sorry. I'll be praying for you."

"Thanks." Tyler reached for a cookie and stared at it. "What am I going to do, Joe?"

Joe selected a cookie for himself, trying to organize the jumble of thoughts in his head. "Doris has the best first idea."

Tyler laughed. "Yeah, man, I've been praying. This whole time. I'm not sure what God's trying to accomplish with this."

"That's an understandable feeling. Seriously. But you know God's bigger than us, right? We don't always get to understand everything right away." Joe bit into a cookie. It was probably a little rich for him to say that to Tyler. Between the two of them, Ty had more years as a strong believer that Joe, despite their age difference.

"Yeah. I know. I wish . . ."

"I think we all do." Joe reached for a drink and sipped. "But let's start there. Let's pray—right now. I've been learning to ask for guidance and understanding rather than just assuming I know everything already."

"You?"

"I know, right?" Joe grinned. "I can't promise, obviously, but I think it's going to be all right, Tyler. Look at me. I'm fifty-five. I've only ever really loved one woman and I thought she was lost to me. But now she's back in my life, and it's like those missing years never happened."

Tyler nodded, then looked away.

"What?"

"It's just—I don't want that. I don't want to lose the best years of my life because of this. I want marriage. A family. I realize it sounds mean, and I'm sorry, but you're old. I'm glad you found Cynthia again. She seems cool, and the two of you are good for each other, but dude, so what?"

Tyler's words were little bullets, ripping into Joe's heart. He pushed down the hurt. The kid was dealing with a big loss. Even if it wasn't permanent, right now it felt like it would be. Joe could cut him some slack. "You're not wrong. And I'll be praying that you don't have the same losses that I have."

"Joe. I didn't mean—"

"It's okay."

"No, really. I'm just—"

"Tyler. Let it go. Eat your cookie and then let's pray, okay? And if you want to hang out here tonight, you're welcome."

"You don't mind?" Tyler stuffed the rest of the cookie into his mouth before reaching for another.

"Of course not. But only if you don't mind hanging out with old people. Cyn's coming for dinner."

Tyler paled and he started to speak with his mouth full.

Joe shook his head. "It's all right, Ty. Nothing you said was wrong."

But all of it hurt more than Joe would have said was possible. Had he wasted those years? Was there any point in trying to reclaim them?

~

"DR. MITCHELL?" Dr. Curtis poked his head in her office door. "Do you have a minute?"

"Sure, come on in." Cynthia smiled at the young doctor and swiveled away from processing her Monday morning email glut. "What's up?"

He sat across from her and folded his hands in his lap. "I've been watching you the last couple of weeks. You seem happier."

She laughed. "I guess I am. Although, I don't think I was unhappy before."

"No. Oh, no. I didn't mean to imply that. I was just wondering if there was a reason for it?"

She tilted her head. "What are you getting at?"

"Okay. I know how you feel about gossip."

She nodded. It hadn't taken long for her reputation as one who had no tolerance for the scoop that floated around the hospital like a small town full of yentas. "But?"

He blew out a breath. "But people are talking about you and Mr. Robinson. It's not good."

"I'm not doing anything wrong."

Dr. Curtis waggled his hand from side to side. "He's still your patient, isn't he?"

"Actually, no. Not that it's any of your business. When I realized that we both still had feelings, he transferred to another doctor in the practice."

His eyebrows lifted. "When was this?"

"It's been at least a month. Why?"

"I'm not sure how much credence to give it, but the nurses are saying someone is lodging a formal complaint. With the hospital board."

That wasn't good. The board cared about one thing, and one thing only: appearances. Oh, sure, they wanted the best doctors and good recovery metrics, but none of that mattered if they couldn't also get donors. And that meant a squeaky-clean image. Instinct warred with a desire to know more. She needed to know, though, didn't she? If she was going to be able to defend herself. "Do you know who?"

"No. I can probably find out . . . ?"

Cynthia closed her eyes. This wasn't what she wanted to be worrying about. Her patients needed her full focus. And yet, they needed her here, too. Employed at the hospital. Which she wouldn't be if the board decided her love life was a detriment to the hospital's reputation. "Would you?"

He nodded, looking relieved. "Only because it's you. I appreciate how much you've taught me. You're a good doctor. You don't deserve this."

She managed a slight smile. People rarely deserved anything they got—good or bad. "Thank you. And . . . I appreciate your bringing it to my attention."

He stood and paused at the door. "You might want to suggest he steer clear of the hospital. I think the fact that he's been picking you up has been feeding the rumor mill."

Of course it had. Because no one loved gossip more than people who worked at a hospital. "You're right, of course, and I'm not sure I would have thought of it. Thank you."

"Dr. Mitchell?"

"Yes?"

"Don't let this get to you, okay? You always say it's the patients who matter. Keep that your focus."

"Definitely." When he'd left, closing the door behind himself, she slumped against the back of her chair. Rumors and innuendo seemed to cling to female doctors. As enlightened as the larger world pretended to be, the medical world was still basically an old boys' club. She'd learned to keep her head down and do her job while ignoring the little digs. How many people assumed she was a nurse simply because she was female? She'd lost count. Nurses were amazing—and not all of them were female!—but their functions were different. And that was just part of it.

Was she willing to sacrifice some of her reputation for a relationship with Joe?

The question sounded dramatic in her head. Except it wasn't. Not really. Dating someone who had been a patient— even though he wasn't one any longer, nor would he be again— was going to raise eyebrows and garner whispers behind her back.

Did she care?

That was something she was going to have to think about. To pray about.

Cynthia was convinced that God had brought Joe back into her life. That part wasn't really in question. But was it just so that she could help him physically and he would remember his faith? Or were they going to be able to find their way to one another in a more permanent way now that they were older?

The alarm on her phone chimed. She'd have to worry about Joe later. She was meeting with two members of the hospital administration in ten minutes and needed to start the trek over to that part of the building. When she'd gotten the meeting request, she hadn't thought about it at all. She was new-ish to the staff. Everywhere she'd worked before had wanted to touch base fairly frequently with new doctors to see how they were settling in and make sure all was as it should be. It wasn't always —or even usually—the administrators, but Cynthia had figured this time it was because she was higher up in the department.

Her gut twisted.

Thanks to Dr. Curtis' visit, she was pretty sure they were going to talk to her about Joe. After a moment of thought, she wiggled her mouse and clicked over to the email conversations she'd had with Joe's new doctor when they transferred his case. She hit print, frowning as the printer on her desk whirred to life.

It was possible she wouldn't need the documentation.

But it was likely that she would.

10

J oe pushed away from his desk and stood. He shook his arms then raised them over his head, sighing a little when his shoulders and back popped. Cynthia nagged him about making sure he got up and moved around every hour, so he'd set an alarm. He'd grudgingly admit—to himself only—that she was right. It helped.

He rolled his head on his neck and crossed from one end of his office to the other, making horizontal X's with his arms then stretching them out as far as he could.

There was a knock on the door and he bit back a groan. "Come!"

"Sir?"

Joe's eyebrows lifted and he flipped through his mental file of employees. "Christopher, right? Come on in. What can I do for you?"

The young man swallowed, his Adam's apple bobbing. He exuded nerdiness with his thick black glasses and full, scruffy beard. "I was wondering if we could talk about Captain Collins."

"Captain . . . who's that?" Joe gestured to the more casual

seating area in the far corner of his office. "Do you want a drink? There are sodas in that mini fridge."

"Sure. Thanks. Can I get you something?"

"Why not? There's diet lemon lime, I think. I'll take one of those." Joe sat in one of the arm chairs and waited for Christopher to join him. He popped open the can, sipped, then looked at the man who, according to reports that he was now remembering, was the best software engineer in the government services division. "You were telling me about a captain."

"Collins. She's the PM on several of contracts I'm also on. I'm not sure about her actual title in the company—we're government services?"

"Yes." Joe nodded and grinned. "I pieced it together."

"Sorry, sir. I should have been clear up front."

"You're fine. Call me Joe, would you?"

"I—Joe, sir?" Christopher blinked several times, almost like he was assimilating new information, then he nodded. "I'll try."

"So is this Stephanie Collins? Is that who you mean?"

Christopher nodded.

Joe sipped his soda. She'd been a captain in the Army before joining the company, but rank had no place here. "Does she ask you to call her that?"

"No, si—Joe. But she doesn't have to. It's like we're all privates and she's there to whip us into shape. It's part of what I wanted to talk to you about. No one can deny she's a great project manager—that's not a question at all. She's very competent."

Joe nodded. "That's good to hear."

"She's just, well, kind of a horrible human being." Christopher's cheeks blazed red. "At least at work. She might be a great person outside of work. But no one knows."

"I know you all have the common floor reserved every Friday afternoon for community building. She doesn't join you?"

"No. And she's pretty adamant that no one on her projects

should be going. Even if your work's done. She says there's always more that we could be doing and that it's not a good corporate policy to encourage loafing around on company time. And, well, some of the guys—they're not all men, we're all coders and, oh boy."

Joe chuckled. "I'm not going to write you up for non-inclusive language. Just be sure the women on the team aren't actually offended by being considered, generically, part of the guys. So, others on the team are . . ."

"They nominated me to say something to her about it. And I tried." Christopher looked down at his soda can and fiddled with the tab. "It didn't go well. She said she was writing me up. So I wanted to come up and talk to you before that got up here. I love this job. I don't want to have to find something else."

They couldn't afford for him to go find something else, either. Not if what Joe was remembering about Christopher's assignment load was correct. They'd be in a real lurch. And while Joe didn't think Christopher was threatening to walk, it was definitely something to keep in mind. "What do you think would be the ideal solution?"

Christopher blew out a breath. "I mean, we're not the Army, right? Most of us can't do more than five pushups."

"She's not asking you to do pushups?"

"No." He chuckled. "But I bet she would if she thought she could get away with it. It's her whole demeanor. She's brusque and bossy and always knows she's right. To be fair, she often isn't wrong. It's just that there are other things we could consider that are also not wrong. But if it was her idea, she's going with it. No matter what."

Joe nodded. "So more open to team feedback?"

"Yeah, I guess that's how to put it. And just . . . I mean we're all on the same team. It's not a military squad. We're programmers. It wouldn't kill her to come play ping pong some Friday afternoon. We get a lot done when we're hanging out on that floor—even if it's not during our specifically scheduled time. And the open hours? There's a woman on your computer security team who has crazy good ideas that we've been able to incorporate into some of the deliverables for the government contracts." Christopher shrugged. "And that sort of collaboration has to be defended vigorously. And even then we sometimes get written up."

Joe leaned forward, elbows on his knees. "I haven't seen any write-ups. So if she's saying she's writing you up, she's not doing anything with them that I'm aware of."

"Really?" He visibly relaxed. "Because I figured I had to be on my last leg with you. I wasn't sure if you were going to even give me the chance to resign or if you'd feel you had to fire me."

"I'm not firing anyone." Although he was definitely going to have to talk to Stephanie. He'd hired her himself and been very impressed with her. Maybe he'd put her too high up starting out, but she had the qualifications. "I'll talk to Stephanie and try to get this sorted out. It would be good for you—and the whole programming team—to remember that she has a lot of experience that we need. She's a decorated combat veteran, too. So while you may see her as bossy, it's probably that she's used to giving orders and not inviting discussion. It's something she can work on, but you can, too."

"Sure. Of course. We just would like to have a more cordial relationship with her."

"Understood. Like I said, I'll have a chat with her. I appreciate your coming to see me." Joe stood.

Christopher followed suit, clutching his soda. "Thank you."

"Any time. My door's always open. At least metaphorically." Joe reached for the door and pulled it open. He followed Christopher out into his admin's area and watched as the young man headed toward the bank of elevators. He glanced over at his admin. "Marla?"

"I must have been away from my desk."

"Oh, that's fine. He knocked. Different question."

"Shoot." She leaned back in her chair and folded her hands in her lap.

"If you were going to have to talk to an upper level manager about their ability to connect with their team, would you do that in your office or theirs?"

"Stephanie Collins?"

"You know Christopher?"

"No. But she's the only one I hear rumbles about. They call her 'The Captain' and I don't think it's intended as a compliment."

"More than just her immediate team?"

"Oh, yeah. Pretty much everyone."

That didn't bode well. "Why didn't you say something?"

Marla sighed. "It was on my list for the day you had your attack. I haven't felt like it was important enough since then."

"Fair enough. But you know I always want to know these things. Gotta keep my finger on the pulse."

She chuckled. "You got it. When I saw you had company, I transferred your phone out to me. Cynthia called and asked for you to get in touch as soon as you could."

Joe frowned. They were supposed to have supper tonight—rescheduled from earlier in the week. In fact, now that he stopped to think about it, she'd been putting him off since Monday. "I'll do that. But Stephanie. My office or hers?"

"I want to say yours—give her a little dose of intimidation, but you're probably better off going to her. You don't want to lose her."

"I don't. We need her."

Marla nodded. "Go to her. Call Cynthia first."

Joe chuckled and gave a two-fingered salute before heading back into his office. He slipped his cell out of his pocket and tapped Cynthia's contact. Would he get a hold of her, or would this be another round of phone tag that ended with her cancelling their plans?

Again.

Cynthia frowned at her cell as it buzzed on her desk. Joe. Of course he was calling back now. She checked the time—she had five minutes, if she was okay running to her appointment. She picked up her phone and tapped Accept. "Hi, Joe."

"Hey. Marla said you called. Sorry about that—meeting with one of my guys that I hadn't planned on. What's up?"

"I'm running around today, too." She clamped her phone between her cheek and shoulder as she rifled through the files on her desk to find what she needed to take with her. "I was wondering if I could just meet you at the restaurant tonight. Maybe we could push to seven?"

"At least you're not cancelling. Yeah, sure. Seven is fine." His words were clipped, his voice cool.

She didn't have time for this right now. She huffed out a breath. He didn't understand any of this. She'd fought too hard for her career to derail it. He was busy at work, too! "Would you rather we shifted to tomorrow night? I can swing out to your place after work instead?"

"No, that's not what I want. I want to see you. I've wanted to see you all week, but you're pulling away, and I don't understand it."

"I'm sorry. That's not what's happening." Was it? She shook her head and collected her stack of papers before heading out the door. "It's just busy for me right now. I can do seven. Text me where, okay? I'll see you there. I really have to run."

"I love you."

"You too. Text me, okay? See you tonight." Cynthia ended the call and broke into a jog. The very last thing she needed to do was arrive late to the department case review meeting. She checked the time. She might just make it.

A handful of people still milled around outside the conference room when Cynthia rounded the corner and slowed to a more dignified fast walk. Not late.

She slipped into the room, nodding to her colleagues as she slid past them on her way to a seat at the table. Cynthia didn't want to intrude on any of the clumps of people talking. It wasn't that she was aloof. It was just better not to get entangled too deeply with coworkers. She'd made that mistake early on. But work friends weren't the kind of friend you shared secrets with—even though they tried to say they were. She'd learned that the hard way, too. So now, she courted being called "not a team player" or "hard to get along with."

There really was no way to win.

So she focused on not losing.

The meeting was about as boring as expected. Meetings were important, she couldn't discount that, but it also didn't mean she had to enjoy them. Her own presentations were well received with the barest minimum of feedback.

Nobody mentioned Joe.

She'd been wondering how she'd handle it if they did. It helped that he was completely past the hospital follow-up now, and solely a patient of the private practice she was attached to. It also helped that she'd made it clear she was no longer his doctor.

She shouldn't have had to, but so it went.

With this meeting out of the way, maybe the rumors would

be put to rest and she could move on without her personal life being used to call her professional capabilities into question.

She loved Joe.

Like him, she'd never gotten over their relationship, though she'd tried.

But she loved her job, too. God had given her the skills and heart to help people. She didn't—wouldn't—question that. And Joe? She still wasn't sure what God planned there. She was trying to stay in the present rather than looking for a future that might not come.

Paperwork and patients filled the rest of her day. When she finally shut down her computer, it was ten minutes to seven.

She was going to be late.

She wanted to go home, change into pajamas, and eat ice cream in front of the TV. The sound of Joe's voice when they'd spoken this afternoon stilled her hand as she reached for the phone. He'd be beyond annoyed. The reality was, this week had been full of cancellations—she owed it to them both to go.

She tapped out a quick text letting him know she was on her way but would be about ten minutes late.

Thankfully, traffic wasn't horrible and she pulled into the valet area only a few minutes behind the time she'd told Joe to expect her.

Joe was already seated and working through a plate of what looked like fried calamari when the hostess escorted her to the table.

"Hi. Thanks for waiting."

His eyebrows lifted, and he gestured to the appetizer. "I didn't. Help yourself, though. It's good."

She nodded and slid into the booth across from him. He was still so handsome. And he still had a poker face that would win tournaments. "What's wrong, Joe?"

"Why should anything be wrong?"

Cynthia fought the urge to wince at his super reasonable tone. She didn't want to fight tonight. Or ever, really. Fighting was never something she chose. She'd do it, but only when it was important. So she'd let it go. "Okay. I haven't been here before. Do you have a recommendation?"

"I usually get the filet." He shrugged and reached for another piece of calamari. "You might like the stuffed chicken. It sounded good when I was looking at the menu."

"That does sound good." Cynthia opened the menu and scanned for the chicken. Stuffed with spinach, artichokes and cheese. More fat than was necessary, but she couldn't face a salad. She pointed to it and waited as the server took Joe's filet order and walked away. "How was your day?"

"Busy. I've got two of my best employees butting heads."

"Isn't solving interpersonal conflict a little bit below your pay grade?" Who took something like that to the owner of the company? And why hadn't Joe sent him back down to whoever was a better choice for dealing with that? HR, maybe?

Joe laughed and, for the first time that evening, his eyes lit. "It is. I don't think it occurred to Christopher that it would be. He's not in possession of the world's best social skills."

"Thus the interpersonal conflict." Cynthia scooped calamari onto a small plate.

"Actually, no. Or not entirely." Joe frowned. "It probably factors in. But Stephanie has some personality quirks of her own. She was a captain in the Army—medically discharged— and she seems to want to run the software engineers like a tactical squad."

"He called her 'bossy,' didn't he?"

"That was one of the words. Why?"

Cynthia leaned back and studied Joe. Was he really that clueless? "Because that's the word men trot out when they have a problem with women in authority."

"I don't think—"

"Of course you don't. You're a man. So when you come across as forceful, people say you're determined and know what you want. When a woman does that, they're bossy—or another b word—and authoritarian. And so, women have to decide what they're going to do. Do I learn to coerce people to do what I need to have done, but in a way that they think it was their idea? Or do I weather the storm of being considered one of *those* women?" She shrugged. She'd tried it both ways. "Sometimes you can find a middle ground, but not always."

"Hmm. I never pegged you as a feminist."

She laughed. "This has nothing to do with feminism and more to do with women who work in a man's world figuring out how to be allowed to be good at their job."

"You've managed it."

"It doesn't always feel that way. For example, I doubt very much there would have been anything more than a snickering 'attaboy' if a male colleague resumed a relationship with an old flame who happened to have been his patient. Certainly he wouldn't have been dragged into a meeting with the hospital administrators." She bit off the words. She hadn't been planning to say anything about it. It had been handled.

"You mean us? This? There's a problem with this?"

"No." She waved her hand. "Forget about it. I dealt with it."

"I'm not even your patient."

She smiled. "I know. Let it go. But just . . . be kind to Stephanie—that was her name, right? If she's coming from the military, she's had to be 'one of the guys' to survive and be taken seriously. It might take her some time to adjust and realize that the software engineers are going to listen to her without her having to prove she has the biggest muscles."

Joe looked like he was going to speak, but the server

appeared with their drinks. When she'd moved off, he reached his hand across the table.

Cynthia rested her fingers in his.

"I'm sorry you ran into trouble at work because of me. I don't want to lose you because of something like that. If there's anything I can do—"

She squeezed his fingers and cut him off. "There isn't. It's handled. I promise."

He held her gaze, and she melted inside. Even if this was a bad idea—and how could it not be?—she loved him.

She always had.

She just wished there was a way to be sure a future with him was something attainable.

11

J oe ignored the buzzing of his cell phone and frowned at the spreadsheet. A quick check of the formula in spreadsheet said the numbers were right, but that made it worse. Some day he was going to grow a stiff enough spine that when a business friend approached him with a failing company, he'd say he was sorry and walk away.

Social media. He scoffed. Why people needed to shout about their personal lives on the Internet wasn't something he was ever going to understand. Everyone assured him it was vital in today's economy, but the numbers for PhotoBuddies sure didn't support that.

Maybe it was the stupid name?

He sighed and pushed away from the desk. It was too late to change the company name. They could try and rebrand—a new logo, some better marketing—maybe that would bring people and advertisers over to the platform. But if it didn't work, he'd have six thousand employees—give or take a few—who would need new jobs.

"Joe?"

He turned and laughed when his gaze landed on Aaron

Powell. "You're working late. Did you know I was looking at numbers tonight?"

The man shrugged. "Word gets around."

Maybe it wasn't surprising that a social media company was big on sharing news. "How'd you get the short straw?"

"I volunteered, actually." Aaron flashed the million-dollar grin that made him one of the best customer-experience managers they had. Aaron, at least, would be easy to slot into any of the other companies if Joe ended up having to shut down PhotoBuddies. "How bad is it? Upper management isn't saying."

"It's not good." Joe gestured to his desk. "New accounts are down by almost twenty percent. Advertising is basically non-existent. I was mulling a rebrand, but maybe it would be better to see if there was a buyer out there looking for something to absorb or spin off. I don't know."

Aaron nodded. "I didn't think it was *that* bad. Rebranding might work, but some of the developers were talking and they had an idea about additional functionality that would give us a competitive edge."

New functionality cost money. And time. And if people weren't already clamoring to use the service, how would anyone find out about it unless he sank more money into advertising the platform. "I don't know, Aaron."

"Could we write up a proposal?"

"Yeah, okay. But I want a realistic proposal. Cost, time, projections—all of it. Not a sales pitch, a reality-driven explanation of how this is going to save your company. Because I'm not sure that's possible. I need growth to start happening six months ago."

Aaron winced. "Got it. No sales pitch."

"Maybe a little one." Joe held his thumb and forefinger a tiny space apart. "But mostly cold, hard facts."

"When do you need it?"

Joe squeezed the bridge of his nose and thought through his calendar. This week was busy—full of meetings. "How about next Friday?"

"The thirtieth?"

Was it already the end of October? He nodded. "If that'll work. I realize it's only a week and a half, but I really would like to start getting a plan in motion to stop the money hemorrhaging."

"Sure. That makes sense. We'll do our best."

"Do we need to have a meeting?"

Aaron paused, as if thinking, then shook his head. "We'll shoot you the proposal. If, after that, you'd like to go over it in person, let's schedule something."

"All right." Joe glanced at his desk where his phone had started buzzing again.

"I'll let you get that. Good night. Thanks."

"Don't thank me yet." Joe reached for his cell as Aaron closed the door behind him. This was the sixth time Cynthia had called tonight. He accepted the call and tried to smile. "Hey, Cyn."

"Hey yourself."

She sounded mad. He frowned at the screen saver on his laptop. "Did I forget something?"

"Dinner?"

"We had plans?" He specifically remembered not making plans with her for tonight because he had such a backlog at work. He wasn't supposed to be working this much, but everything was coming to a head. Work had to get done.

"No." She sighed. "No, we didn't have any. But I'd hoped you would get in touch to make some. I haven't seen you since Sunday."

And even that hadn't been long. He'd made it to church, and they'd had lunch, but he'd begged off spending the afternoon together. Work again. His attempts to shovel out from under the pile of tasks that collected while he had been sick weren't working and the stress was eating away at his ability to sleep at night. "I'm sorry. I miss seeing you, too. I don't think I can swing anything before Friday."

"Because of work."

She hadn't phrased it as a question. Did he need to answer it? "I'm responsible for the livelihoods of a lot of people. I don't exactly sit behind my desk twiddling my thumbs all day."

"No. I know that. I have a busy career, too. But I'm making room for you in that. I thought we agreed that was what we were doing? Because we understand now what we didn't when we were younger?"

He closed his eyes. He *did* understand. He understood that he wanted a life with Cynthia—that he loved her. He also understood that he had responsibilities that he couldn't up and walk away from. So did she! If she was going to walk away when work got busy, maybe he was better protecting his heart now, before it shattered him. There were people counting on him now, more than ever before. "I want you in my life, Cyn. That hasn't changed."

"But?"

He scrubbed his hand over his face. What was he supposed to say? "Have you eaten?"

"It's nearly eight. Yes, I've eaten."

"Eight?" He glanced at the display on his monitor. So it was. "Dessert then?"

"You're still at your office."

He hunched his shoulders. "I did mention things were busy."

"What's that, a twelve-hour day?"

Closer to fourteen, but he probably shouldn't mention it. And he was going to have to take things home and spend at least an hour, maybe two, before he could call it a night. "About. Do you want to lecture me about it over crème brûlée?

There's a good spot for that two buildings down from your condo."

"I know that one. It's worth changing out of yoga pants?"

"Don't change. They're casual. But yes, it's some of the best I've had. Give me twenty minutes?"

"Okay. I'll see you then. I love you, Joe."

His heart warmed. She hadn't been returning the words lately and he'd been worried. Not enough to bring it up as a topic of conversation. But still worried. "I love you. See you soon."

Joe hit End and dropped his phone into his pocket. He frowned at the spreadsheet again before closing it and powering the machine down. After packing his bag with the bare minimum of what he needed to handle before tomorrow's first meeting, he texted Harold and headed toward the elevators.

CYNTHIA PULLED her car into the parking area at the rear of Joe's Georgetown mansion and stopped behind one of the garage doors. If she was blocking a space they needed to access, she'd move. Knowing Harold, he'd offer to do it for her. After the drive from Tyson's to the city, she'd take him up on it.

Nobody did traffic like the DC area.

That wasn't a positive.

She leaned her head against the headrest and closed her eyes. Joe had offered to have Harold pick her up. Maybe she should have said okay. It wasn't as if she hadn't been letting him before now. Except, after dessert on Wednesday—and if she was honest, a little time before that—it seemed like having her own transportation was a better idea.

There was no point in relying on Joe if he wasn't going to put her, and his relationship with her, in front of everything else.

She jolted a little when someone tapped on the glass.

Smiling a little, Cynthia pushed the door open. "You startled me."

Joe tugged the door the rest of the way open and offered his hand. "I wasn't sure if you were coming in or not."

"Of course I'm coming in. Mario always makes an incredible meal. I've gotten spoiled." She leaned up, intending to kiss Joe's cheek.

He turned his head and their lips met.

The sensation was always startling. So much heat and awareness from the simple act of mouths touching. She melted against him, her hands slipping around his waist. This was home. It always had been.

And it seemed just as out of reach as it always had been, too.

She forced herself to ease back, curving her lips into a smile. "Well, hello to you."

"I'm glad you came." Uncertainty lurked in his eyes. Not everyone would see it, but she knew him. Even after all these years she knew him. And any knowledge she might have lost had certainly returned in the almost two months they'd been back together.

"I am too. And not only because the food promises to be amazing." She slipped her hand in his and gave a gentle squeeze. "Did you talk to your Army captain?"

Joe chuckled and pushed the car door closed. "I did."

Cynthia pressed the lock on her key fob before dropping it into her purse and falling into step beside him as he headed toward the house. "And?"

"And you're probably onto something with your analysis of the situation. I'm not sure how to fix it though. The programming team—and it's not all men, but even the women seem to agree—think she's a tyrant. She pretty much thinks they're all insubordinate and argumentative." He shrugged and reached for the glass French door that led from the patio into the long, skinny solarium that ran across the back of the house, looking into the lush gardens.

"Hmm." She knew what it was to be the odd woman out. To be in charge but have no respect from anyone she was meant to be in charge of. "I hope you can find a way that lets her keep her authority."

"Oh. I wasn't planning on taking that away from her. She's a fantastic project manager—I just might need someone to mentor her some. Help her see that people skills aren't a waste of time."

Cynthia laughed. "I doubt very much she sees them as a waste of time."

"You're right. Sorry. It's been a frustrating week."

"I'm sorry." She looked through a doorway into a room she was fairly certain she'd never seen before. "Do you even go in all the rooms in your house every week?"

He stopped and followed her gaze. "Probably not. The market being what it is right now, it's not the best time to sell and find something that makes more sense. I'll unload this place eventually. Maybe I'll look for a penthouse like you have."

"I hardly have a penthouse." She shook her head. "It's a two-bedroom condo."

He grinned. "Up high. Looking over Tyson's. It has penthouse appeal."

"Yes, well. The penthouse in my building is the top three floors and from what I understand they're asking, the chances of it ever selling are slim to none."

"You'd be surprised."

Maybe she would be. There was a lot about the DC area that was surprising. It didn't have the concentrated population like other big cities, but it was still absolutely a big city. It just took the form of suburban sprawl. "I guess we'll see."

"Are you hungry? Mario told me to let him know when we wanted to eat. He said the meal was flexible."

"I could eat."

Joe nodded and brushed his lips over her cheek. "I'll be right back. Go on in and have a seat."

Cynthia set her purse on a little table in the hall and wandered to the dining area where they usually ate. What was she doing here? She chose a different seat at the table this time. The view out into the garden was soothing in the deepening twilight. It gave the feeling of being cut off from the world. He'd said there was a pool—but they hadn't spent much time wandering the walled-in space behind his mansion. It was probably another area he didn't visit with any regularity. But he had to spend his money on something, didn't he?

"Here we go. Soup to start tonight. Homemade cream of mushroom to ward off the nip in the air. Those are Mario's words. I didn't have the heart to tell him the A/C was still running."

Cynthia chuckled. "It's nearing the end of October. It *should* be getting cold. Just because summer seems to cling like a toddler with separation anxiety around here doesn't mean we shouldn't start enjoying some fall flavors."

"Fair enough." Joe set a bowl of soup in front of her, then set another at the seat beside her. He sat and reached for her hand. "Let's bless the meal."

Joe's prayers were more moving these days—more heartfelt. Cynthia's heart filled. It was good to see his faith resurfacing. That was the man she'd known and loved.

"Amen." Cynthia picked up her spoon and sampled the soup. "Mmm. Mario has a way."

"He does."

She studied him over her next spoonful. There were the beginnings of circles under his eyes. "You're pale."

"I'm fine."

"How many hours are you working every day, really?"

Joe's lips twitched down. "As many as I need to. I'm getting up every hour to move around. I'm taking longer walks each day at lunch. I'm fine."

"And that doesn't answer my question." Or did it? Because the only reason she could come up with for him to not be willing to give her a number was that the number would be too high.

"Probably close to eleven. Happy?" He scooped his soup rapidly into his mouth.

"Joe." She blinked back the tears that burned her eyes. She wasn't going to play dirty and cry. Nor did she want him to see how much it mattered to her. And yet, she hadn't been able to keep the censure from her voice.

"I know, Cyn, I do. But there's a lot to do, and the buck stops with me. I'm trying to hand things off, but for every one thing I manage to shake, I get three more dumped in my lap."

"I'm trying to understand. To sympathize. But your health is more important. You have to know that."

"I know I don't want to talk about it."

Heat washed over her at his words. They were a rebuke. A harsh one. She nodded. "Fine. I'm sorry I care."

"Really, Cyn?"

She shrugged and finished her soup. "Shall I go tell Mario we're ready for the next course?"

"I'm not finished yet."

She stood and picked up her bowl. "There's room enough on the table for an empty dish. I'll be right back."

She hurried from the room. In the formal dining room, she slowed and peered through doorways until she found the kitchen. "The soup was delightful, Mario. Thank you."

"I'm glad you enjoyed it. Did Joe not finish yet?"

"We were talking." She smiled, ignoring the burning in her gut. "I'm sure he'll be finished when I get back with the entrees."

"I can bring them. You're a guest."

"Surely we're past that by now." She slipped around the counter and set her bowl in the sink. "I don't mind and I'm sure you have other things you want to do with your Friday night."

"There's dessert yet. I have an apple pie in the oven, and I made vanilla ice cream this afternoon. No sugar in either—I'm curious to see what you think of them."

"They sound delicious."

Mario deftly plated sliced chicken breasts on what looked like wild rice. "Are you okay?"

"Me? Yes. Of course."

He shook his head. "You don't have to tell me, but I don't believe you."

She sighed. "I'm just struggling some. Joe's . . . Joe."

Mario chuckled. "He is. This is the most relaxed I've ever seen him, if that helps you any. And having permission to fix more grownup meals has been wonderful."

At least Joe was taking some of the lifestyle changes seriously. It wasn't just his heart she worried about. Her own heart was also at risk. "I, for one, am grateful you're not only willing but capable. The ones I've sampled have been delicious."

"If it's not too bold, I'm going to put it out there that his heart attack is the best thing that could have happened to him."

She frowned.

Mario leaned closer. "It brought you into his life. He's changed. For the better."

"I'm glad to hear it." She smiled and reached for the plates. Did she believe Mario? That was a question, for sure. She believed he was serious. That he meant what he said. And she could even point to changes she'd seen in Joe.

But were they enough to risk her heart again?

12

"Thanksgiving is in three weeks."

Joe nodded at Stephanie across the conference room table. He could have held the meeting in his office as it was just the two of them. From the way she was bristling, he decided the more formal setting had been the right choice. "I'm aware of that."

She crossed her arms. "I'm not sure how, exactly, you expect me to turn a morale problem around in three weeks. Especially when it's not *my* morale problem."

"Isn't it? They're your team."

"Subordinates."

"*Team.* And I believe we've found the crux of the problem." He sighed and pinched the bridge of his nose. "Stephanie, this isn't the Army. This is a solutions provider that contracts solely with the government. No one questions that you are an exceptional project manager. You have fantastic rapport with the customer—especially when we're talking to bigwigs at the Pentagon. You know what they want. You know how to express to them that we understand their needs. And you've improved their satisfaction with our deliverables."

She nodded. "I wasn't aware you knew all of that."

"Of course I do. This company has a flat management structure on purpose. I never want to be thought of as a figurehead sitting up at the top of an org chart, completely out of touch except for what I hear from two or three people."

She nodded again. "I guess I don't understand the problem."

"Our developers—*your* developers—hate you."

She bristled. "I'm not here to make friends."

"Of course you're not." Joe pressed his lips together to keep himself from muttering anything else unprofessional. Did she even want to be here? He took a sip of water and studied her. Her cheeks were flushed—anger was more likely than embarrassment—her expression stony. "Regardless of whether or not you want to make friends, you can't continue to treat the dev team the way you have been. I can replace a project manager. I can't replace an entire division of programmers."

Stephanie stiffened. "I think the reports you've heard may be exaggerated."

He shook his head and fought a sigh. "I don't. They've been forwarding me your emails. A few have recorded your visits to their side of the office and sent them along. There's nothing overtly wrong with your management style, but we may be at a point where we need to decide if it's compatible with our corporate culture."

She paled. "You're firing me?"

"No. And I don't want to. I want you to fix morale before Thanksgiving." Joe squashed the tendril of pity he felt for her. It had to be hard to hear. And yet, shouldn't she have known this was coming? It wasn't as if the developers were quiet about their frustration. "Tyler Shaw—have you met him?"

She gave a slight nod.

"He's going to help. I understand it's going to be change.

Probably a hard change. But I also believe you can do it. You're an asset to the company. I want to see you succeed."

"Yes, sir." She shifted in her chair and started to stand. "Is that all?"

"Yeah. That's all. I'll be checking in as well."

"Looking over my shoulder."

"Don't think of it like that. This is a growth opportunity."

She snorted and started toward the door.

"I'm serious, Stephanie. This is going to help everyone in the long run."

She just lifted a hand as she walked through the door without looking back.

That hadn't gone as well as he'd hoped. Before Joe could organize his thoughts for the next meeting, there was a tap on the conference room door and Tyler poked his head in.

"Do you have a minute?"

"Sure." Joe gestured for Tyler to come in. His eyebrows lifted when Tyler shut the door behind him before taking a seat. "What's up?"

"Was that Stephanie Collins?"

"Yeah. They're having some morale issues."

Tyler nodded. "I've heard. You handled it?"

"I hope so. But now I'm wondering if I did. How'd you hear?"

Tyler shrugged. "You know how programmers talk. It's come up in a few meetings when I've been trying to coordinate and consolidate IT resources. I was going to bring it up with you next time we had a review."

Joe sighed. He hadn't actually intended to drop in and see how things were improving. Usually the threat was all it took to get people to shape up. "I guess I'll keep an eye on it. I don't think it's all Stephanie."

"Oh, no. It isn't. Chris is amazing at his job, but he doesn't make it easy for her to do hers."

"Did we make a mistake hiring from outside?" Stephanie had all the right qualifications, and she'd proven herself to be an asset, but maybe they should have promoted Chris. Would there be this kind of drama if they had?

"No. We need her. She's good." Tyler laced his fingers together. "I didn't actually come to talk about that."

"Sorry. Of course. Tell me."

"It's Danielle." Tyler frowned. "I got an email from her. She wants to come back to work."

"Already?"

"It's been almost two months. Physically, she's doing very well."

"I hear a 'but.'"

Tyler nodded. "She still doesn't remember that we were dating."

Joe winced. "Maybe being back in the office would help? If she can come back, if she remembers how to do her job, we need her. We're supposed to push out a big update in March and she's the best at UI design. We probably have people who could make it work, but if she's able to come back, I'd rather have her."

"Yeah. Of course." Tyler dragged a hand through his hair. "All right, I'll let her know."

"Shouldn't that be HR's job?"

"Oh. Probably. She emailed me. Maybe that's because I've been around? I think maybe she thinks I'm just a designated work contact. I'll let HR know, then. Thanks, Joe."

"Anything else? That equipment audit went okay?"

"I mean, you know how those are. I'll have a report to you by the end of the week."

"Bottom line?"

"We need to purchase some stuff. I'll include recommendations as well. Most is for the contract with DoD we just won."

Joe nodded. They'd built new equipment into the cost of that proposal. "That's good. Get me the report, and we'll go from there. Thanks, Ty."

Joe gathered his laptop and papers and followed Tyler from the conference room. He had about thirty minutes before he needed to leave for an onsite lunch with one of their clients. In his office, he dropped his computer on its dock and glanced around when he heard buzzing.

His cell.

He'd left it here when he met with Stephanie because he hated when people were trying to sneak peeks at their buzzing devices when he was talking. Lead by example and all that.

Six missed calls.

He winced as he scrolled through. Cyn was definitely trying to reach him. No voicemail though, so maybe it wasn't important?

He tapped her contact and then the speaker button so he could continue to gather what he needed for the meeting and then finishing up at home.

"This is Cynthia Mitchell. If this is a medical emergency, please hang up and dial 9-1-1. If you need to have me paged, please dial the hospital at 703-"

Joe ended the call and slid his phone into his pocket. He'd try again later if she didn't call him back.

Bag in hand, he paused by Marla's desk on his way out. "I'm heading to my lunch meeting, then I'll finish from home. You know how to reach me if you need to."

She smiled. "Have a good rest of the day."

"Thanks. You, too. If Cynthia tries the office line, would you transfer her to my cell?"

"Of course. See you tomorrow."

He lifted a hand and headed toward the elevators, running through the tasks he needed to finish before he called it a day.

He made a mental note to call his parents around dinnertime. They needed to firm up their Thanksgiving plans.

Would Cynthia join them? Hopefully she could. They needed to talk about what her schedule was going to look like over the holidays. He'd love to take her to Florida for a few days. They could visit his parents and spend some time on the beach away from everything. Or as "away from work" as he ever managed to get.

She'd probably have something to say about that.

But he wasn't the only one who had a hard time answering the phone.

Was it too late? Were they both too set in their ways—too committed to their careers—to have a chance at making something work between them?

CYNTHIA CHANGED into comfy flannel pants and a long-sleeved T-shirt. She tossed her work clothes in the dry-cleaning bag in the closet and sighed. She hadn't been home on a Friday night in nearly two months. She'd known better. She shouldn't have gotten used to having something to do. Someone to hang out with.

She and Joe had played phone tag all week.

Oh, they'd managed a few short conversations, but they'd been interrupted when one or the other of them had to run. It was breaking her heart.

Yesterday, when she hadn't been able to get a hold of him all day—though to be fair, he had tried to call back and she'd been busy—she'd texted that she wasn't going to make their standing date tonight.

He'd begged over text and had tried to call, actually leaving several voicemails, but she'd stood firm. She needed to figure out what was going on. The one benefit of age was under-standing that sometimes it was okay to take a step back and pause. It wasn't the end of the world.

It shouldn't be, at least.

She padded down the hall and into the open kitchen and living area. She should eat. Her stomach twisted. Nothing sounded good. Still, she opened the fridge and pulled out a container of yogurt. Good enough.

Carrying it and a spoon, she moved to the couch and tucked her feet under her before hitting the power button on the TV. There probably wasn't anything good on, but she could always find a movie to stream if she got desperate. For now, she just wanted the noise.

Maybe she should get a cat.

Her phone rang and she closed her eyes. She didn't want to talk to anyone. Especially not Joe.

She wasn't on call. And yet . . . she reached for the phone and frowned at the display.

"Hello?"

"Cynthia, dear? It's Louise, Joe's mom?"

"Hi, Mrs. Robinson."

"I think we're past that now, honey, aren't we? I was hoping you'd finally agree to use my first name."

"Of course. I'll try. How are you? How's Florida?" Cynthia scooped a bite of yogurt and muted the television.

"Oh, warm as ever, though we've got a nice breeze off the water tonight. I called over at Joe's. He'd mentioned that the two of you usually spend Friday nights together."

Her stomach sank. "Mrs.—Louise. I just couldn't make tonight work."

"Joe seemed to think it was more than that. Are you getting cold feet?"

Cold feet? As if they were engaged or something? "It's not

that."

"I'm glad to hear it. Will you be coming to Thanksgiving? Originally, Dennis and I thought we'd come up there, but Joe was saying he thought the two of you could use a little time away from the office. We'd certainly love to have you if you can make it. I think Joe is going to convince Mario to come down as well. It's not usually a hard sell. That boy loves the beach. So can we plan on you?"

"Thanksgiving?" Her mind was racing. The idea of spending the holiday weekend in Florida was a lovely one. Warm sun, sand, surf—what could be better? But could she make that plan now when she wasn't convinced there was any point in trying to prolong this attempt at a relationship? It wasn't fair to anyone to keep trying to pretend. Not when she knew it wasn't going to work. "I'm not sure. I'm low man on the totem pole at the hospital. I may not be able to get the days off."

"Oh." Disappointment oozed out of the single syllable. "I hadn't thought of that. You're such a well-known and well-respected doctor. I thought for sure you could take holidays."

Louise wasn't wrong. It was entirely possible that, if she were to ask, she could easily get Thanksgiving off. But it wouldn't be fair to pull rank. And it was easier than explaining the situation in detail to Joe's mom. "I'm sorry. I'll see what I can do and talk to Joe. I appreciate the invitation."

"Our door's always open."

"Thank you. And thanks for calling, it was nice to hear your voice. Have a good night."

"You too dear. Bye now."

Cynthia ended the call and dropped her phone back on the coffee table. She scraped the last of the yogurt out of the tub and, after a moment, just turned the TV off.

She couldn't go to Thanksgiving with Joe.

Not when she knew she needed to end things.

13

"You're a hard woman to get a hold of." Joe pointed to the empty seat beside Cynthia in the sanctuary. "Is this seat free?"

"Sure." Her smile was faint, almost strained looking. "How are you feeling?"

His eyebrows lifted. "I'm doing fine. You can always check with Dr. Stevens if you're worried."

She stiffened. "Did your mother mention she called me?"

"She did." Joe reached over and covered her hand. She didn't push him away, but she might as well have. He sighed. "You really can't come?"

"Joe. I just don't think it's a good idea."

"Good morning everybody!" The overly cheerful praise band leader boomed into the mike. "Let's stand and worship the Savior!"

Joe stood. He glanced at Cynthia as she slowly rose to her feet. The guitars opened into a rollicking intro to the first song and he leaned close to be sure she could hear. "What's not a good idea? Thanksgiving?"

She gave her head a slight shake.

"Then what?"

"Joe." She frowned and seemed to come to a decision. "This. All of this. I can't do it. You're still the same man, Joe. You care more about your work than anything else. And I'm not much better, though I feel like I try. But we're both too in love with our careers to ever make space for someone else. I love you, Joe. I always have. But I can't be with you anymore. I deserve someone who will put me first, even when they're busy, and I don't think that's ever going to be you. I'm sorry."

She might as well have slammed a boulder into his chest. He couldn't quite draw a breath. He was staring at her, mouth agape, and none of the signals from his brain were making it to his muscles. "Cyn."

She shook her head and stared at the words on the screen, singing quietly.

Joe swallowed. She'd dumped him. In church. What was he supposed to do now?

One thing he wasn't going to do was make a scene. Another was sit next to her for the next ninety minutes knowing that she'd ended things. He turned and picked his Bible up off his seat and, muttering "excuse me," made his way to the aisle. He paused and let his gaze linger on Cynthia for a moment—just long enough that she seemed to deliberately not look his way.

Right. He plodded up the aisle to the foyer and glanced around. Harold had said he wanted to attend the service today. Joe wasn't going to disrupt that. He slipped his phone out of his pocket and stared at the screen. He could call Tyler. But that would mean having a conversation, and he just didn't have the words.

So. A taxi.

He tapped the button to call and made his way out into the cool November air. A taxi could take him home. Or. He drummed his fingers on his leg before tapping another contact on his phone.

He'd head to Florida now. There was no reason he couldn't work remotely. If people needed to see him, he'd fly them down. Or he could fly up for the day. It was what, a two-hour flight?

Joe paid the taxi and stepped onto the curb by the terminal for private planes. He glanced around. Doris should be here already with his bags. He scanned the area.

"Joe!" Doris waved from beside a column.

He strode across the distance and smiled. "Thanks, Doris."

"I think I got everything you'll need, but if I missed something you let me know. I can either send it down, or I guess you can just buy it new." She shook her head. "But I'm also not sure this is the right move."

That was the problem with treating staff like family. They felt like they could have opinions on his personal life. "When you're losing a war, you retreat, Doris, before the casualties get any higher than they already are."

"Maybe the problem is that you're treating love like a battlefield."

He shrugged. "Maybe so. Then again, I'm pretty sure there are no fewer than six songs that make the same comparison. So I can't be completely wrong."

"Joe." She frowned and crossed her arms.

"I know. Trust me, I get it. But she made herself clear, and I'm not going to push."

"Every woman wants a man who's going to fight for her."

He chuckled. "Do they? Seems to me that that's considered sexual harassment."

"I'll concede it's a fine line, but I don't think running at the first sign of trouble qualifies."

"Doris, you're the world's best housekeeper—and you do so

much more than simply keep my house clean. You know I value and respect you, right?"

She nodded.

"Then please, because I love you and you love me, butt out."

Doris laughed and shook her head. "Fine. But know that Harold, Mario, and I are all rooting for Cynthia."

"Fair enough. But if I catch any of you wearing a shirt that says 'Team Cynthia' in my presence, we're going to have words." He leaned in and kissed her cheek. "Do you and Harold want to come for Thanksgiving, too? Mario's cooking. Some Florida sunshine is bound to be needed by that point. And you know my parents adore you."

Her cheeks pinked. "I'll talk to Harold."

"Things are finally serious between you two?"

"Joe?"

"Yeah?"

"If I'm butting out of your personal life, I'll ask you to do the same."

He laughed and held up his hands. "All right. Just let me know when the wedding is. I want to come."

"You'll be the first. Now get going. Pete said they're cleared to take off whenever you need. He took everything onboard already, except for this." She gestured to a small rolling bag with his briefcase hooked to the top. "I figured you'd want it in the cabin."

"You're a gem."

"Safe trip."

"Thanks. Let me know about Thanksgiving, okay?"

"I will. Do you want Harold to come down this week so you have a driver?"

"Believe it or not, I know how to operate a car. Figure out something else to worry about. I'll be fine." Joe snagged the handle of the suitcase and waved before turning to stride into the airport.

It wasn't a lie. He would be fine. He'd been fine ever since he and Cynthia broke up in college.

He'd been hoping there was more to life than that. Loving Cynthia and actually having her in his life was like a dream come true.

Now he'd go back to living without the one person in his life who mattered more than anyone ever had.

He'd done it before.

He could do it again.

It'd be fine.

Just fine.

"Happy Thanksgiving." Dr. Curtis set his tray down on the four-person table in the far side of the hospital cafeteria and tilted his head to the side. "Can I join you?"

Cynthia scooted the stacks of folders she'd brought with her out of the way and gestured to a chair. "Why not? How's it going?"

"Good. Mostly good. I was hoping to get Thanksgiving off, but at least this way I get Christmas." He sat and pulled the tray closer. "Plus, this smells pretty good."

"For a hospital Thanksgiving dinner, it's not bad."

"I'm kind of surprised you're working today."

"I volunteered." She'd had three offers from people at church, but the thought of taking anyone up on it had sat wrong. Surely everyone there had seen her sitting with Joe. And then seen her *not* sitting with him. She didn't want to talk about it. This was easier. "It seemed like the right thing to do, being new here."

"Well, it won you some points with the nurses. Or so I heard."

She shook her head and stabbed at the last green beans on her plate. "You're going to want to get over your addiction to gossip. I know it's fun to be in on what people are talking about, but it can bite you in the rear if you're not careful. I'd hate to see that happen to you. You're a young, promising doctor."

Red blazed a trail across his cheeks and he stared down at his food. After a moment he cleared his throat. "There's this one nurse. Do you know Jessica?"

"Sure. She's—oh." Cynthia chuckled. "I see. So it's less about the gossip and more about spending time chatting with her?"

He nodded.

"Well, I'd still encourage you to steer conversations away from that, when you can. Get to know her as a person, not as an information source."

"I thought I might see what she's doing tomorrow. She's not on the roster and neither am I. Since I couldn't make it home for the big meal, I convinced my folks to just wait for Christmas. But now I don't know what to do with my free time."

"It's a commodity, for sure. Why not just go walk around the monuments? It's chilly, sure, but not so cold that you'd be miserable if you wore a jacket, maybe got some coffee or hot chocolate to carry around with you. That'd give you plenty of time to talk. And there are a ton of fun restaurants if you stretch it into dinner."

"You think she'd go for that?"

Cynthia smiled and tried to remember if she'd ever been that young and unsure. "I would have. Honestly, I still would. To me, it sounds like a date where your focus is spending time together. Most women prize that."

"Okay." He cut into the slices of turkey on his plate. "Then I'll ask her after lunch. It's better than a movie. That's all I could come up with, but I hadn't seen anything listed that sounded interesting."

Cynthia had been looking at the movie listings herself that morning. There wasn't anything that reached out to grab her attention, either, but it was better than another evening alone in her condo. And maybe she'd stroll through the mall. If nothing else, it would be exercise. If she was lucky, it would get her thoughts off Joe for more than two minutes at a time.

Hanging out with Joe. Playing Scrabble. Kissing in front of the fire . . .

"Are you and Mr. Robinson doing anything fun this weekend? I bet he's unhappy you had to work."

"Well. I guess it's interesting to see where the rumor mill failed. We're not seeing each other anymore. I'm not sure what his plans are." She didn't even know where he was. She'd driven past his house in Georgetown three different times, even though she'd known it was stupid. It hadn't looked like he was home. Then again, the place was so large, he could be in any number of rooms and there wouldn't necessarily be lights visible from the street. But the gate in the back had been shut, and even the garages looked empty. "I'm sure he'll have a lovely day."

"I'm sorry. It's not because of work, is it?" Dr. Curtis frowned. "It seems like our job gets in the way of relationships a lot."

"Lots of doctors manage. Nurses, too." She took in his earnest expression and shook her head. "I think it boiled down to wanting different things. Or different expectations. One of those. Maybe, after a certain age, you can get too set in your ways to be able to make room for someone else in your life."

"I don't think that's true. I'm not sure what kind of faith you have—maybe none, which is okay too—" He broke off and frowned. "I'm botching this. But I think if God wants people to be together, He'll arrange it. Of course, we have to not mess it up —'cause He'll let us do that, too."

She nodded. She'd been praying about her relationship with Joe, hadn't she? Certainly at the start. And then?

The food in her stomach turned into a hard, hot ball that twisted greasily.

Had she been so focused on the time they each spent on their jobs that she'd missed how well they'd worked a relationship into it? It wasn't as if she'd expected either of them to not have other responsibilities. That wasn't reasonable. And yet that was almost exactly what she'd expected of Joe. The man ran five successful tech businesses. Of course, he was busy! But he'd stepped back. He'd made room.

And she'd thrown it in his face.

Cynthia closed her eyes. What had she done?

14

"Well, I still can't believe you didn't at least call her to wish her a happy Thanksgiving." Joe's mom frowned at him as she filled his coffee cup and then her own. She set the carafe back on the warmer and sat beside him at the breakfast bar.

Joe took a sip and looked out over the water. The house had been a bit of an impulse buy, but when it came on the market, it was too good to pass up. It was only two houses down from the house he'd bought his parents when they decided to retire to Florida. The area was good for tourists too, so he could always turn it into a vacation rental if he decided to base himself more permanently in DC again. Or he could do the split-year thing. Missing out on the DC winters, even though they tended to be mild when compared to someplace like Michigan, wouldn't be a bad thing.

"Are you listening to me, Joe?"

"Hmm?" He dragged his thoughts away from the waves and looked at his mom. What had she said? Calling Cynthia. "Mom, I can't call her. She dumped me before we got to the chorus of

'Good, Good Father.' She doesn't care if I hope she has a happy Thanksgiving. She wants me out of her life."

"I just think—"

"Don't think. It didn't work out in college, and it's not going to work out now." The words burned in his gut, but that didn't make them untrue. He'd give anything to figure out how he was supposed to run a successful business—or five—and do more than he had to make room in his life for a relationship. "I'm not sure what her expectations are, but they're more than I can meet. I can't always promise I'll leave work at five. Or be free for lunch. Honestly, I'm surprised she can. I guess at the end of the day, we're too different."

"That's the thing, honey, you're not. You're exactly the same." Mom sipped her coffee and studied him. "I suspect that's the bigger problem. Let me ask you this, and then I'll stop."

Joe sighed and reached for his mug. "Okay."

"Do you love her?"

Joe closed his eyes. Leave it to Mom to cut to the chase. "I do. I don't think I ever stopped. Not really. Having her back was like a miracle."

"Aha."

"No, Mom. There's no 'aha.'"

"Joe." She waited until he looked her way just like she had when he was fifteen. "Are you praying about what God wants? Not you. Not Cynthia. But God?"

"Not when you say it that way, no."

"Maybe you should be." She patted his shoulder, drained her coffee, and stood. "I'm going to head back to our house. Your father's probably anxious for some waffles about now. I hid the ones Mario made and left for us. Are you sure you shouldn't have asked him to stay longer?"

Joe smiled. "He deserves a vacation, too. He'll be back in January. He's been talking about this foodie tour of New Zealand with some of his friends from culinary school for months. I'm looking forward to whatever new recipes he picks up."

"Won't it be cold? December isn't exactly warm."

"New Zealand, Mom. It's summer there."

"Right. Of course." She smiled and shook her head. "Well, I hope you'll come to dinner tonight."

"I have a fridge full of leftovers, but I might anyway, just to have another chance to see you and Dad."

Mom laughed. "Right. When will you be heading back up to DC?"

"Probably next week. The company Christmas party is in two weeks and there are always a few last-minute details that I end up needing to handle."

"You should invite Cynthia."

He closed his eyes. He'd planned to, originally. Had toyed with the idea of proposing to her afterward. It would have been fast, sure, but it wasn't like they were starting from zero. They'd been on the brink of marriage thirty years ago. He'd loved her all those years in between. She'd said the same. Why wait any longer? "I don't think that's a good idea."

"Joseph Andrew Robinson." She stood with her hands on her hips, her lips turned down into a scowl.

He hunched his shoulders. He couldn't help it—the response was ingrained. "Mom."

"You love her. She loves you. At your age, you should be done being an idiot. Fight for her!" She threw her hands in the air and let out an exasperated sigh. "Pray first. But your father and I both think the two of you belong together. We've been praying for this day for years. Honestly, I would've liked it better if you'd gotten back with Cynthia when grandchildren were still a possibility, but even without them, this is the woman God designed for you. I know it. Dad knows it. And I think, if you stop and listen to what the Holy Spirit is whispering in your heart when you pray, you know it. So stop being stupid and fight."

When the kitchen door clicked shut behind her, Joe still hadn't formulated a response. Doris had said the same thing: fight. If this was a business deal—one he was sure was right for the company—he'd fight. So why wouldn't he pursue Cynthia?

Because he was hurt. That was part of it. Her words had sliced holes in places he hadn't realized could bleed. But that would heal. Especially if he could get her back. So why wasn't he trying?

Fear?

Joe drained his coffee. He stood and walked over to the picture window that looked out over his private beach. Sometimes fear was healthy. Sometimes God used fear to keep people from making big mistakes.

But sometimes, the devil used fear to keep people from pursuing God's plan.

Joe grabbed his windbreaker from the hook by the door and stepped out. He'd walk on the beach, pray, and plan.

Because if God wanted Joe with Cynthia, he wasn't going to mess it up.

Not again.

CYNTHIA SIGHED as she settled in her usual spot in the sanctuary. The Christmas decorations were minimal, but lovely. Garlands swooped between sconces down the sides of the room, each festooned with poinsettia leaves and holly berries. A tall tree stood at the edge of the platform. Sparkling white lights wound around the boughs. An advent wreath with tall, purple candles stood in the center near the pulpit.

She liked the focus on Advent. This was the second week.

She glanced at the program she'd taken as she came in and nodded. Faith. That was a good focus for the week. She needed to remember it.

It had been three weeks since she'd spoken to Joe. Three weeks since she sent him away. But only a week and a half since she'd realized the enormity of her mistake. She'd almost called him every day since Thanksgiving.

But what was she supposed to say?

"Is this seat taken?"

Startled, Cynthia glanced up. Her jaw dropped. "Joe?"

He lifted his eyebrows and pointed at the empty chair.

"No. No, help yourself. You're back in town." Ugh. Could she sound any stupider? Of course he was back in town. He was sitting next to her. Which begged the question: *why* was he sitting next to her?

"It's good to see you."

She opened her mouth to speak but the praise band filed onto the platform and asked the congregation to bow their heads. She did. But she snuck peeks at Joe through the whole prayer. When the prayer ended, they launched straight into the same song they'd played three weeks ago. The one she'd talked through, telling Joe to leave.

Heat washed over her. This couldn't be happening!

Joe stood beside her, singing as if nothing was wrong. His hands were at his waist, palms up in the not quite willing to raise them but needing to do more than stuff them in his pockets posture he usually took.

What was he thinking?

She was hyper-aware of him beside her. All through the singing, the lighting of the second Advent candle, and the sermon. It took effort to focus on the pastor's message on faith— trusting God even in the darkness.

Had God brought Joe back?

Would she get a third chance to do things right?

When the service was over, Cynthia took a deep breath and touched Joe's arm before she could chicken out. "Will you come for lunch?"

"I can't today. Thank you. I did want to give you this." He held out an envelope with her name in calligraphy across the front.

"What is it?"

"Open it and see." He smiled and some of the tightness in her belly eased. "I have to run. Harold's waiting. It was good to see you, Cyn."

Words jumbled against each other in her brain as he stepped into the aisle and the leaving crowd carried him away from her. That hadn't gone at all like she'd imagined their first time seeing each other would. Maybe the more dramatic reunions were on the ridiculous side, but surely he could have said more than fifty words. Agreed to have lunch. Or asked for a rain check. Something that would indicate he was as sorry about their breakup as she was.

What if he wasn't?

Cynthia looked at the envelope in her hands. Shaking slightly, she slid her finger under the flap and pulled out the fancy card inside. She drew her eyebrows together and flipped it over.

A Christmas party? At Joe's company.

Black tie.

She smiled. This was her chance to let him know how sorry she was and win him back. Step one? A killer dress.

It was time to go shopping.

15

"Thanks for coming out to the house, Tyler. Take a seat." Joe gestured to the sprawling dining room table that he'd turned into a workspace. Stacks of files sat at each place. They were organized—to him at least—but he still needed help with the final decisions.

Tyler hesitated before pulling out the chair next to Joe and sitting. "What's going on?"

Joe leaned back and tented his fingers. This was the first time he was going to say it out loud. His heart was on the verge of racing, but a little healthy fear was good, right? He took a deep breath and shot up a quick prayer that if this wasn't what God was leading him to do, He'd use Tyler to make it clear. "I'm thinking of breaking up the company."

Tyler stiffened. "I'm not sure I heard you right."

"You did." Joe smiled slightly. It was a natural reaction. Especially given that from Tyler's point of view—or anyone's, for that matter—it seemed sudden. And ominous.

"What does that mean, exactly? Break up. Not shut down."

"No. Not shut down. And I'm not walking away, either. I'll still be here to help when people need me. But lately it's been made clear to me that work has consumed my life. I'm not sure that's how it's supposed to be. I need a better balance."

"So take a vacation." Tyler frowned at the stacks of paper on the table. "Tearing apart your life's work isn't going to give you balance."

Joe chuckled. "I thought about that. A vacation. Maybe even a leave of absence. I don't think it's enough. Besides, I don't want to completely quit working. I'm not retiring. We're restructuring."

"Restructuring is a more promising term." Hesitation and uncertainty filled Tyler's voice. "Tell me what you have in mind, and I'll try to keep from interrupting till you're done."

"All right." Joe stood and paced the length of the table while he spoke. "The company is made of five arms. Five major areas of focus. Each one of those could be its own company—in fact, two of them used to be, before I bought and absorbed them."

"Because they were failing." Tyler muttered under his breath. He held up a hand. "Sorry. Done interrupting."

"You're not wrong. But they're doing okay now." Mostly. The social media arm was on shaky ground, but Joe believed it could be salvaged. Their plan was promising, at least. "Everyone has areas where improvement is needed. The way we're structured now, it's up to me to identify and address those areas. If I don't see it—or if you, or someone more closely involved doesn't bring it to my attention—they can go unnoticed for too long."

Tyler nodded.

That was promising. "I take responsibility for that. I hoped that keeping a flat leadership structure would be a good thing— and it does have its positives—but it's also caused some problems. Giving each individual arm more autonomy can help with that."

"Only if there's good leadership at the helm." Tyler flipped open the folder in front of him, and his eyebrows drew together. "This is my résumé?"

"You're a couple of steps ahead of me. You're right, yes, that they'd need good leadership. And beyond that—since being in charge of a company the size of any of the five is going to have the potential for amassing a lot of personal wealth, as well as a tendency to overwork, whoever we choose to head up a branch needs to have a solid personal life. One that isn't easily discarded when work gets busy."

Tyler cocked his head to the side. "You're playing matchmaker."

Joe cleared his throat. "I wouldn't phrase it quite that way."

"I would." Tyler tapped his folder a moment before sliding it aside and laughing. "The fact that Danielle's folder is directly under mine seems to support my theory."

"Okay, fine. Yes. I want to help nudge our candidates toward marriage. I regret . . ." So much. Joe bit his lower lip and shook his head. All the years he and Cynthia wasted. So many opportunities lost. "Anyway. I don't want to put someone in the position where they can make the same mistakes I did."

"Is marriage one of the requirements for taking over a branch?"

Joe returned to his seat and put his elbows on the table. "I mean . . . yes. But I don't plan to tell them that."

"You're not going to tell them." Tyler shook his head. "How exactly do you think you're going to keep it from them?"

He grinned. "I'm going to make it a contest."

"A contest."

"Yeah. We're going to choose the two people we think are most suited to run each branch. We'll look at their reviews, productivity, all the stats. And then, when it's all said and done, we'll choose one man and one woman to be in the running for the job."

"What if someone declines?"

"I don't think they will. But we'll keep that in mind when we're choosing our contestants. I think we can probably figure out who wouldn't be up for it and just rule them out in advance. I'm planning to announce this at the Christmas party—"

"That's in ten days!"

"I know. That's just the announcement. We'll start the contest January first, and it'll run through June."

"Do you think six months is enough for people to fall in love and want to get married?"

Joe sighed. That was a trickier question. "Maybe. They're all old enough—I don't have a folder for anyone who isn't close to thirty. Or older. They're not kids. They know who they are, at this point. And we're not choosing any couples who haven't worked together for at least a year. So they know each other. This isn't a blind date."

Tyler ran a hand through his hair. "I'm not sure we should be messing with people's lives like this."

"I'm not forcing them to get married."

"But if they don't, can they take over the company?"

"I might make them work together indefinitely. I guess I haven't thought that part through all the way. Can't we cross that bridge when we get to it?"

Tyler closed his eyes. "Just for grins, let's say we get through June and the two applicants are equally qualified, equally desirous of the position, and they hate each other. What will you do?"

Joe sighed. "How likely do you think that's going to be? Surely one of them will show a little more aptitude?"

Tyler shrugged.

"I'll deal with that if I have to. Worst case? I'll just not restructure that permanently and reabsorb the running of it under my umbrella." It wouldn't be ideal. The goal was for Joe's load to lessen.

"You're going to get bored."

He laughed. "I don't think so. I'm going to start a charitable foundation and focus my efforts there. Without everything else on my plate, I should be able to keep that to standard business hours."

"Not if I know you." Tyler chuckled. "But I like that you're going to try. This is weird, Joe."

"Good weird or bad weird?"

"You know, against my better judgment, I'm going to say good weird. Just weird enough that it might work." He paused and studied Joe before adding on, "Does this mean you're back together with Cynthia?"

"It means I'm working on it."

"Good." Tyler nodded and patted the folders in front of him. "Let's figure out our other four matches."

"Four?"

"Well, Danielle's the one for me, whether she remembers it or not. So if you're offering one of these jobs to me, she's the only one I want in the running. She knows her stuff."

"Business apps?" Joe scribbled on a sticky note and offered it to Tyler.

"Yeah. Sounds good." He took the sticky and put it on his folder. "What's next?"

Joe grinned. This was going to be fun.

"THANK YOU, HAROLD." Cynthia stepped out of the car Joe had sent for her and glanced at the glowing stone front of the St. Regis Hotel. Joe certainly knew how to throw a fancy party. The venue alone added buckets of class she wasn't sure she was equal to.

"Always a pleasure, Cynthia. I'm glad you came." Harold stepped back and nodded toward the door.

Joe strode towards the car, looking at home and heart-stoppingly handsome in his tuxedo. She'd only seen him on Sundays —last week and the week before—and he'd begged off lunch each time. Cynthia had worried he wasn't going to give her a chance to explain. Or at least apologize. But she clung to the invitation like a lifeline. She was here tonight, and he would have to let her talk.

"Hello, Joe. Thank you for sending Harold." She brushed at the skirt of her beaded midnight blue gown. She'd agonized over the color—it was a Christmas party, so maybe red or green would have been more suitable. Or black. Black was always right for formal affairs. But the beaded gown with illusion sleeves and V-neck had caught and held her attention. So she'd gone with it. It was a fairy tale dress for a date with the man she realized was her very own Prince Charming. If he'd let her tell him.

"My pleasure. I'm sorry I couldn't come, too. There were some final details that I had to see to in person." His gaze roamed over her. "You're stunning."

Her cheeks heated. "Thank you. I could say the same."

He laughed and offered his elbow.

Cynthia slipped her arm through his, but halted his forward movement. "Joe. Before we go in, I want to say I'm sorry."

"No. I'm sorry. I wasn't honest about my work hours with you. I didn't even try to explain or have a conversation about it. You don't have anything to apologize for."

Her heart sank. What did that mean? She shook her head. "No. I do. I let my fear get the better of me, and I said things I didn't really mean. I love you, Joe. I always have. Please tell me I didn't lose you for good."

He pressed a gentle kiss to her temple. "You didn't. You're making my life a little easier though."

Cynthia chuckled as the tension in her body dissipated. "So you forgive me? We can go back to where we were?"

"I forgive you." He kissed her again. "I love you. Now let's get inside before all the mini eggrolls are gone."

He didn't say anything about resuming their relationship. But maybe he just thought it was understood. She was here with him now. That was all that mattered. It was all that would matter.

She barely noticed the opulence of the lobby as they made their way through to the ballroom. Glittering chandeliers hung from the ceiling. Servers in black made their way through the groupings of elegantly set tables to offer food and drink from gleaming silver trays. And the people. Joe's employees might trend on the nerdy side, but they knew how to dress for a party.

"Do you have to own a tux to work at one of your companies?" Cynthia nudged him with her elbow. "Everyone certainly cleans up well."

Joe laughed and leaned close. His breath tickled her ear and neck, sending shivers down her spine. "It's not a requirement, but it helps. Most of the time, after their first Christmas party, people invest. Although my admin says the women will rent their dresses. I guess that's a thing?"

"Sure." She nodded. She'd considered it after her third dress store. If she hadn't found something at her fourth stop, she might have looked into that. "That way you're not locked into the same dress year after year. Men can get away with that. Women not so much."

Joe shrugged. "I don't think I'd notice, to be honest. Although, I also wouldn't mind seeing you in this dress more than once. Did I tell you that you take my breath away?"

"Not in quite so many words."

His lips brushed her cheek. "Well, you do."

Cynthia let go of his elbow and slipped her arm around Joe's waist instead. His arm came around her shoulders and she tucked herself close, savoring the heat of his body next to hers. "This is quite the party."

"They work hard. They've earned it." Joe scanned the crowd, then turned to meet her gaze. "Would you like to dance?"

They danced and laughed and then found a table where Cynthia met Tyler Shaw again. It was good to see him looking as happy as he did, though he kept staring at the table where Danielle was seated with members of her team.

The meal was as elegant as the rest of the setting. No rubber chicken with rice pilaf—the staple of medical conferences. The filet was tender, the new potatoes crisp on the outside and creamy in the middle. As the servers began to clear the dinner dishes in preparation for dessert, Joe squeezed her hand under the table.

He stood and tapped his spoon handle against his water glass. The room quieted. One of the servers appeared behind him with a microphone. "Good evening, everyone. Thank you again for a wonderful year. You've all worked hard to get us to where we are, and I expect that to keep happening as we go forward."

People around the room chuckled.

"Some of you know—or, seeing how the office grapevine works, maybe all you know—that I reconnected with my college sweetheart in September when I had the good fortune to be taken to her hospital when I had my heart attack." There was another smattering of laughter. Joe glanced down and her and held out his hand.

Cynthia's heart started to race. She put her hand in his and, when he tugged gently, rose and stood beside him.

"This is Cynthia Mitchell. The love of my life. I've lost her twice now, and that's not something I want to have happen a third time. And so, starting in the new year, I'll be doing what she's strongly encouraged me to do since I was twenty years old: getting a life. Part of that is going to involve stepping back from some of my responsibilities at work, although I don't want anyone to panic. I am and always will be available to all of you. I've always been proud of our corporate culture. I don't want that to change. We will, however, be restructuring. Each of our five individual corporate arms will be transitioning to more independent entities. Which means I'm going to need five new Senior VPs."

It was as if the whole room drew in and held their breath. Cynthia looked around at the faces of Joe's employees. No one seemed alarmed—they were mostly curious. She turned to watch Joe as he outlined the basics of the competition that would be starting in January.

She didn't know much about running a multi-billion-dollar company, but this didn't seem like a typical way to go about . . . anything. Not that Joe tended toward the typical.

"There will be a company-wide email with more details on Monday. And if you have questions or concerns, my door's always open. I believe, firmly, that this is only going to benefit every one of you going forward." Joe flipped the mike upside down and flicked the switch before holding out Cynthia's seat and taking his own. He turned to face her, a tiny smile playing on his lips. "What do you think of my Christmas present?"

16

J oe fought the urge to fidget as Cynthia stared at him.

"Your Christmas present?" She frowned and started to shake her head. "I don't want you to break up your company because of me. That's just a bad idea, Joe."

"I'll have more time away from work. More time for you. For us." His stomach twisted. Had he seriously miscalculated? "When you got here, you asked me if we could go back to where we were. That's not what I want."

"Oh." Her face paled and her shoulders sagged. "Of course not. It's a lot—"

He grabbed her hand. "I want us to move forward. I love you, Cynthia. I'm asking you to marry me."

She just sat there. Blinking.

In for a penny. Joe dug into the pocket of his tuxedo pants and withdrew the ring he'd had made for her as soon as he'd gotten back in town. There were three rows of channel-set diamonds that made up the band and a double row of them circling the larger center stone.

"Joe." Cynthia reached for the ring. Her gaze flicked back up to his. "It's gorgeous. Can you—"

"Afford it?" He grinned and slipped the ring on her finger. "I think we'll be okay."

Cynthia held out her left hand and admired the ring before cradling his face in her hands. "I love you."

"I love you. I'm hoping since you haven't taken that off and thrown it at me, you're saying yes?"

"I'm saying yes." She leaned forward and their lips met.

Joe sank into the kiss, tugging her closer so he could wrap his arms around her.

There were a few claps. Then more joined in. Soon, applause filled the ballroom, punctuated by sharp high whistles.

Laughing, Joe eased back and rested his forehead against hers. "I forgot we had an audience."

"A big one." Cynthia brushed her lips across his once more before scooting back into her seat. "You still didn't have to break up your company for me."

"It's time. I think this is going to be good for everyone. Me included." Joe prayed it was so. The last ten days of planning with Tyler had gone well. Smoothly, even. They hadn't argued over the choices, even though Joe had expected to. "It's not going to be immediate. This contest will take a lot of time for the next six months. It might get busier before it gets better."

"I understand looking at the long game, Joe." She covered his hand. "I appreciate you doing this for me. For us. You're not going to be bored?"

He laughed. "No. Like I said in my speech, I'm still going to be around. It'll just be a more advisory role. And I was thinking about starting a charitable foundation. The company isn't particularly organized with its benevolence, and we should be. If nothing else, from a tax standpoint we should be doing more, but I also think we're missing opportunities that we wouldn't if we had a formal foundation."

"That's a big undertaking."

"Not when you consider what I'm stepping back from." He held her gaze. "I'm working toward a Monday to Friday, nine to five. That's my goal."

"I can't promise you the same."

"I'm not asking you to. Your hours are already reasonable. This will give us more time together. And it'll mean I can plan vacations I actually take." He paused and cleared his throat. "About that."

"Vacations?"

He nodded. "Apparently we have a vacation home in Florida now."

She laughed. "Of course we do."

"It was there and the price was right." Although he hadn't really looked at the price that carefully.

"Then I can't wait to see it."

His heart soared. "What sort of wedding are you hoping for?"

"Give me a couple of days to get used to being engaged, would you? This ring was a lot of years in the making."

"All right. But don't take too long, we've already wasted so much time."

Cynthia stood up and held out her hand. Couples were filling the dance floor and the DJ had switched to a slow love song. "Come and dance with me so we don't waste any more."

Smiling, Joe took her hand and led her to the floor. He tugged her into his arms and held her close. There were a billion little details to handle, but they could wait.

He and Cynthia could handle them together. As a team.

Forever.

EPILOGUE

S tephanie Collins watched as Joe and his apparently new fiancée took to the dance floor. She crossed her arms and fought a scowl. What did he think he was doing, breaking up the company? He'd lost his mind.

Well, his stupidity was going to be her gain.

She'd improved morale in the government services division. Or at least in her part. Maybe the rest hadn't been suffering from problems in the first place. Not that her team should have been. They were all whiners. None of them would last a day in the Army. But she knew how to play the game—at least once she figured out what the game was. If the civilian side of things needed Stephanie to be soft, sweet, and motherly, then that was what she'd be. She could bat her eyelashes at the software engineers if that got them to stop mucking around and do their jobs.

But she shouldn't need to.

It wasn't going to matter.

This was her shot—she wasn't sure what would be involved in being selected to be part of the competition to take over the government services division, but she'd do whatever it took.

She let her gaze roam over the tables full of her laughing

coworkers. None of them had invited her to sit with them. That was fine. She wasn't there to make friends.

Stephanie stopped when she reached Christopher Ward. He could fill out a tuxedo surprisingly well. His broad shoulders would even do justice to dress blues. Toss in his sandy brown hair, boyish smile, and the fact that he willingly wore the same style of frames the Army issued that were jokingly referred to as birth control glasses or BCGs and, well, he made work a little more visually appealing that it would be otherwise.

Not that she was interested.

He was a pain in her backside. He'd been the one to go to Joe and get her in trouble in the first place.

She pressed her lips together.

He might be handsome. He might be funny. But he wasn't her friend.

He was the enemy.

It would be smart to remember that.

WANT A FREE BOOK?

If you enjoyed this book and would like to read another of my books for free, you can get a free e-book simply by signing up for my newsletter on my website.

ACKNOWLEDGMENTS

People sometimes ask me where I get my ideas. Well, this one came from a joking conversation with Valerie Comer over Facebook Messenger one night. And then, it kind of lodged in my brain and I thought...what if?

And that's really the germ of all my books. That what if.

In this case, I definitely owe a huge thank you to Valerie for encouraging me to write it, even though we were laughing. I'm also grateful to Lynnette Bonner (cover designer extraordinaire) and fabulous friend and for the amazing editing of Lesley McDaniel. I'm still not sure I would have followed through on writing this series were it not for the invitation to be part of the Love's Treasure Collection. So thanks to Juliette Duncan and Autumn Macarthur for that!

First, last, and always I'm grateful for Jesus and for my family. My husband, Tim, who is as introverted as I am and so also considers the time we spend on the couch together at night doing our own things quality togetherness. And he also gives me time to write outside of that whenever needed. I'm thankful to my boys for putting up with the distracted mom look when I'm pondering a plot point. And I'm thankful for my mom who continues to encourage me even though she's with Jesus. She spoke so many words of love and support into my life, that they echo there still today.

Beyond that, I appreciate you. I'd still write without readers, but it wouldn't be nearly as fulfilling.

OTHER BOOKS BY ELIZABETH MADDREY

So You Want to Be a Billionaire

So You Want a Second Chance

So You Love to Hate Your Boss

So You Love Your Best Friend's Sister

So You Have My Secret Baby

So You Need a Fake Relationship

So You Forgot You Love Me

Hope Ranch Series

So You Love Your Best Friend's Sister

Hope for Tomorrow

Hope for Love

Hope for Freedom

Hope for Family

Hope at Last

Peacock Hill Romance Series

A Heart Restored

A Heart Reclaimed

A Heart Realigned

A Heart Redirected

A Heart Rearranged

A Heart Reconsidered

Arcadia Valley Romance – Baxter Family Bakery Series

Loaves & Wishes

Muffins & Moonbeams

Cookies & Candlelight

Donuts & Daydreams

The 'Operation Romance' Series

Operation Mistletoe

Operation Valentine

Operation Fireworks

Operation Back-to-School

Prefer to read a box set? Find the whole series here.

The 'Taste of Romance' Series

A Splash of Substance

A Pinch of Promise

A Dash of Daring

A Handful of Hope

A Tidbit of Trust

Prefer to read a box set? Get the series in two parts! Box 1 and Box 2.

The 'Grant Us Grace' Series

Wisdom to Know

Courage to Change

Serenity to Accept

Joint Venture

Pathway to Peace

Prefer to read a box set? Grab the whole series here.

The 'Remnants' Series:

Faith Departed

Hope Deferred

Love Defined

Stand alone novellas

Kinsale Kisses: An Irish Romance

Luna Rosa (part of A Tuscan Legacy)

Non-Fiction

A Walk in the Valley: Christian encouragement for your journey
through infertility

For the most recent listing of all my books, please visit my website.

ABOUT THE AUTHOR

Elizabeth Maddrey is a semi-reformed computer geek and homeschooling mother of two who lives in the suburbs of Washington D.C. When she isn't writing, Elizabeth is a voracious consumer of books. She loves to write about Christians who struggle through their lives, dealing with sin and receiving God's grace on their way to their own romantic happily ever after.

facebook.com/ElizabethMaddrey

instagram.com/ElizabethMaddrey

amazon.com/Elizabeth-Maddrey/e/B00A11QGME

bookbub.com/authors/elizabeth-maddrey